The Darker Side of the Ferry

Elizabeth Moss

The Darker Side of the Ferry
by Elizabeth Moss

First published 2024

ISBN: 9798346226444
Imprint: Independently published

© Elizabeth Moss

The right of Elizabeth Moss to be identified as the author of this work has been asserted by her in accordance with the Copyright, Designs and Patents Act 1988.

All rights reserved. No part of this publication may be reproduced, stored in or introduced into a retrieval system, or transmitted, in any form, or by any means (electronic, mechanical, photocopying, recording or otherwise) without the prior written permission of the publisher. Any person who does any unauthorised act in relation to this publication may be liable to criminal prosecution and civil claims for damages.

This book is sold subject to the condition that it shall not, by way of trade or otherwise, be lent, re-sold, hired out, or otherwise circulated without the publisher's prior consent in any form of binding or cover other than that in which it is published and without a similar condition including this condition being imposed on the subsequent purchaser.

ONE

How? Why? Where? When?

All these questions were rushing through Julie's mind. She sat on the edge of the hard-sprung bed and looked out the window into a view of endless fog. As she pushed her greying hair away from her face, she saw her reflection in the windowpane. The face staring back didn't resemble her; she had aged and looked haggard. The worried look hadn't left her since her sister, Mandy, had just vanished into thin air six months prior.

Julie couldn't remember when she last washed or coloured her hair, she looked down at her bitten, chewed nails, gone was the beautifully manicured and polished look; vanity meant nothing to her anymore. The detective had said it looked like her sister must have either slipped or she may have been suicidal and had taken her own life by jumping into the river by the jetty. That, she just couldn't or wouldn't believe.

"Either way," he added. "Your sister's body would have been carried out to sea by the strong tidal undercurrent up to the rocky coastline, and maybe she would never be found."

Julie lay back on the uncomfortable mattress and crossed her arms under her head, trying to get comfortable. The room she was staying in, although large, had little furniture.

There was a small television on the wall, and a dark oak bedside table on which sat a dimly lit lamp. A matching old dark oak wardrobe was pushed into a corner and looked out of place. Even a few panels from the oak flooring needed replacing; no one could walk around barefooted. The faded rug had lost its original grandeur of the Fleur de Lys pattern. She'd used the bathroom when she first received the keys to the room, the shower in the bathroom had a small stainless-steel head and the taps squeaked when she tried the water pressure, only allowing a dribble of water to flow. The white sink had seen better days with its limescale finish, and the toilet had a brown wooden seat and overhead flush; it wasn't exactly welcoming.

Julie had gone over and over reading the case, which was now closed until any further evidence of what might have happened to her sister was forthcoming.

Julie had inherited her Mum's tall and willowy looks, which Mandy, her older sister by two years, envied her for. Julie could never understand why, as Mandy possessed her own beauty.

Growing up, their dad was very sickly and spent a lot of time in hospital and always looked extremely pale. He had been adopted, along with their Mum they had both tried to trace the family to try to find out if what he had was genetic and to see if anyone else in his family had suffered from the same ailments. He had passed away in his forties due to a rare blood condition. No medical professionals had known much about it. Julie's mum had hit a brick wall in her research. She had so desperately wanted to have found something about her husband's family or the blood disorder he had inherited just in case either Mandy or Julie carried the rare blood gene, but nothing could be traced or found.

Their mum had died a few years later, making the two sisters even closer. She'd tried so hard to make up for the loss with no father figure, and looking after him day after day had been hard on her. When Julie looked back to those times, she thought maybe their mum had simply died from exhaustion and worry. Her eyes glanced up and looked at the paint peeling from the ceiling.

"Where are you, Mandy?" she cried. "Why didn't you wait for me?"

Julie took the photograph of Mandy from her purse and looked at her sister's pretty face, smiling into the camera. She had her dad's blue eyes and Mum's coppery blonde wavy hair, which gave her a striking look, whereas dad's hair was finer, straight, and slightly lighter in colour. The photo was now dog-eared from the number of times she had removed it from its home in the pocket of her purse as she had stopped to ask passers-by if they had seen her sister. Everyone's reply would all be the same; shaking their heads and saying.

"What a pretty girl, I would definitely have remembered if I'd seen her." It was almost as if the whole village had been given a script.

It was also unfortunate for Julie that here at The Gateway Bed and Breakfast, where Mandy had last been seen, there had been a new turnaround of staff in the last six months since her sister's disappearance. Still, she was here to try and piece the mystery together for herself and maybe she could shed new light on the case, and it would be reopened.

Mandy and she had decided to pick up where their mum had come to a brick wall. Researching the family tree on the internet made things easier than ever. They had wanted to find out if any of their family were still alive, and if so, where?

When their dad had become older his adopted parents had told him which agency they had adopted him from; he had also been told a little bit about his background, which included a couple of photos of himself; one of him at six months old wearing a long white Victorian-looking christening gown, the woman holding him was looking soulfully into the camera. It had startled Mandy and Julie, as the woman had the same intense blue eyes as Mandy.

"Please look after him," was written on the back of the photograph.

When Julie had arrived at The Gateway pub that late afternoon, she was glad she'd booked a room in advance. The place was busy. The three-hundred-mile train journey with many stops and changes, had exhausted her. Although she was living off adrenaline after the arrival, weariness soon set in. Julie was looking forward to a light meal and rest, both in body and in mind.

She felt insecure and uncomfortable as she lay on the lumpy bed, fighting back tiredness and frustrated by the lack of internet and mobile phone signal. Julie had used the pub's telephone, when she had arrived to contact Mandy's boyfriend Paul to inform him, she had travelled to the small hamlet of Duro to try to find out more information about her family and to retrace Mandy's last known footsteps to see if anything more had surfaced here about her sister's disappearance.

But he wasn't answering any calls. Julie hadn't been able to contact him for a few weeks now, so she just left him messages. Of course, he couldn't phone her back as she had no mobile signal at The Gateway or in the surrounding area.

Although the whole place was in dire need of modernisation and a refresh of paint, it had amazed her at the cleanliness of the off-white telephone. It was spotless almost as if it had been cleaned to remove evidence of fingerprints…, but Julie thought maybe she just was being paranoid and overthinking.

Even if something had happened to Mandy, she wouldn't have gone without a fight, and everyone would have known about it. As Julie replaced the receiver, a voice behind her said.

"No one uses the phone that's why it's so clean."

The voice made Julie jump as she turned around. She saw an elderly man; from what she could see of him he was wearing a dark green corduroy jacket which had seen better days and long grey unkempt hair. He was hunched over a local newspaper. *What a strange thing to say,* Julie thought. He carried on talking without taking his eyes away from the tabloid.

"We hear what we need to hear through The Watchers and The Listeners. It's carried by the breeze being sent through the trees." Julie felt slightly creeped out by that. The Watchers and The Listeners?! She remembered Mandy saying.

"Everyone around here catches the No.7 bus from the car park into the village for the latest gossip and catch-ups."

Julie recalled at the time when her sister mentioned that and had taken a mental note to catch the No.7 bus, but Mandy had never mentioned anything about The Watchers or The Listeners. Julie would definitely have remembered that.

She let out a large sigh, breaking the silence around her and bringing herself back into the stuffy old room she was staying in.

Hopefully, by the morning the fog would have cleared, and she could do some of her own investigations. As Julie tossed and turned throughout the night, she kept reliving and thinking about the final months before Mandy had left their deluxe apartment to visit here, the Hamlet of Duro, to find their dad's lost family roots and the long sought answers to their mum's questions.

Technology had changed so rapidly since both parents had passed away; you could almost find anything you wanted on the World Wide Web.

Mandy was a whizz on the internet, her job was marketing, and she knew where to start the research to look for their dad's family. They went to the website of 23andMe, and the Haplogroup reports took them through DNA tracing, carrier status reports, and wellness and traits reports. There were Health Predisposition Reports to help you learn how your genetics can influence your chances for certain diseases.

The Carrier Status Reports could tell you about variants that may not affect your health but could affect the health of your future family. The list went on. As their dad had such a rare genetic blood disorder, which although had not been disclosed, it was quite easy to trace his biological mother and a lot quicker than going through the correct channels of the adoption agency.

"There!" said Mandy, with triumph. "Here is our dad's biological mother. Now, all we must do is go onto another media wall. We will put her name in the search engine and see where it takes us."

They waited with bated breath, as Mandy entered the information.

They weren't expecting it to be that easy, but it was. Their dad's mother, Monica, had four children. She'd had their father, and a daughter adopted, the remaining two had stayed with her.

It appeared Monica came from a wealthy background, but they were very humble and kept themselves to themselves, living off their land. If they were that wealthy, then why have two of her children adopted? That they didn't understand. The land they owned was called The Pastures and was part of Duro.

Their land finished at the bank of the River Duro, and on the opposite side of the river stood a seventeenth century pub called The Gateway, which had survived a fire; the conflagration had destroyed the Great Barn next to it.

The old pub certainly looked as rundown outside as it was inside. It was busy due to the old jetty by the pub car park, where ferries would take passengers over to Duro Rock. The No:7 bus used The Gateway's car park as a pickup and drop off point for the villagers and tourists.

Duro Rock was a few miles from the mainland where monks had dwelled many centuries ago who would help and work at The Pastures for dad's family, cultivating herbs, in the large greenhouses. The produce still grew on the arable land, which their dad's family still owned and were still marketing their products all over the world. Some herbs were frozen, dried and sold for cooking, seeds and oils were sold to health food shops, and others, such as opioids and codeine from the poppy were sold as products to be made into pharmaceutical medicines.

Over time, the monks died out, and a company of whom no trace could be found had bought Duro Rock; the chapel was now used for romantic weddings, and the monastery had been modernised into a luxurious hotel for guests. It wasn't cheap, but it looked out of this world. When not being used for wedding getaways one could take a ferry and visit this breathtaking place.

People came from far and wide to visit Duro, the views from The Rock were picturesque. On the mainland there were so many bird species that twitchers would take the path through the marshlands along from the jetty, just for the scenery alone and to see if they would be lucky enough to catch sight of a Little Crake or a Marsh sandpiper.

But Mandy wasn't looking or reading any further once she'd read about the wedding venue on Duro Rock or The Innis as the locals called it. She grabbed Julie's arm and cried out.

"Oh Yes. This would make the most wonderful wedding venue for Paul and me. It would be sooo romantic."

Marry Paul? She had only known him for eighteen months. The fervency of her excitement took Julie aback. Mandy noticed the surprise and flicked back her long locks of caramel curls.

"It will be fine," she smiled. "We are in love."

Julie nodded and smiled back at her, Paul was great, but she wasn't so sure about him marrying her sister, he certainly wasn't reliable, and she hardly ever saw him.

Julie thought back to the night they had met him. Mandy and she had gone to a local club, it was more like an adult youth centre than a nightclub.

It had become their weekly booze-up. The two sisters knew most of the people who drank there. They were either work colleagues or neighbours who lived in the same apartment complex.

Julie noticed Paul first, his elbow was propping him up against the bar; he was tall, with dark hair and his grinning smile showed a beautiful full set of white teeth. She watched him as he flirted outrageously with the bar staff. His pale blue denim shirt showed off ripped muscles. He was good looking, and he knew it.

Julie pointed him out to Mandy, who watched as he walked over to them, she averted her eyes away from him as if not interested. As always, the guys would try to get to know Julie first to get closer to Mandy, she didn't really mind, and just played along.

Mandy loved the chase, cat and mouse as she called it, but when she met Paul, she fell for him, and within a week they were dating. He had weirdly shown a great interest in their research to find their family tree and took the trouble to follow up on any leads.

Although he was kind and charming you could never track him down or know what he did for work. Mandy adored him; but Julie didn't trust him.

Mandy would often go out of her way to prepare romantic evenings together; she would cook his favourite food, light low lit candles and play smooth music.

Then Julie would be asked to leave the apartment, she would pop across the corridor and have a prosecco evening with their neighbour Angela, her bestie. As usual on her return most evenings Mandy would be sat alone staring at the floor.

"He never showed up." She would sob. Each time she forgave him as he would always turn up eventually with his charm and flowers.

Everything came to a head when Mandy finally found where their dad's family came from and the island of Duro Rock where people could get married, of course, she had asked Paul straight away to marry her and had already planned everything out in her head. She had wanted for the three of them to descend on the hamlet, introduce themselves to the villagers and inform them they were related to the family who once owned The Pastures, part of Duro, and then for the wedding to take place on Duro Rock inviting their friends and family. Paul had laughed and thought she was joking at first. But when he realised, she had meant it and the sincerity of it all, he had pushed her away.

"You can't be serious, Mands," he laughed.

Mandy was devastated and fuming by his rejection.

"How could we possibly marry each other?" he'd said. "It's only been eighteen months; we hardly know each other."

And with that, he closed the door and left. He knew all about me and Mandy, but we knew nothing about him.

The next few days were almost unbearable with Mandy being upset and banging everything around her when she got angry. Everyone who got in her path was a victim of her rants. She knew what Paul had said was true, but Julie thought her sister was in denial.

Mandy and she had planned to go to Duro the following March, but because of the recent upset Mandy had wanted to visit the place straight away.

"C'mon," she had pleaded. "Let's drive down there now, we know now where Dad's biological family came from and Duro reads like a wonderful place to visit. We can stay at The Gateway and take a ferry over to Duro Rock, look around the hotel, and perhaps see if our ancestral family still live in the area and introduce ourselves."

Julie shook her head, knowing what her sister was scheming, she wanted them to go now, hoping Paul would miss her and follow them to Duro.

"I'd rather go next March as planned," Julie replied. remembering her sister screaming back in frustration.

"You are such an old stick-in-the-mud," came back her reply.

Julie recalled trying to calm Mandy down, but this was no longer a discussion.

"It's taken us and Mum when she was alive a good ten years, to track down Dad's family, you never know if either of us has, or is carrying this rare genetic blood and we also need to find out more about it." She ended up taking a pause, showing tears of anger.

"We're still only in our twenties," Julie replied gently, "Another six months isn't going to hurt. Maybe we can find out more info about the area and our family before venturing there?"

Then Mandy got angrier. "It's always later or maybe. Mrs Maybe," she taunted.

Julie went into her room and closed the door.

Mandy and Julie lived together in a large luxury apartment overlooking a park, usually life was great, and they had so much fun, but when her sister got like this it was best to keep out of the way, Julie had grown up with her breakouts and she had learned to just rise above it.

In the morning, Julie got up as usual and left for work. She had crept about the spacious flat so as not to disturb her sister.

During the day Julie thought about how worried she had been about Mandy and had decided to leave work early to pick up a meal for two along with Mandy's favourite bottle of red and a bunch of flowers which contained some purple statice, her favourite colour. Hopefully, it would cheer her up.

She got stuck in work traffic and by the time she had returned to the complex, it had begun to get dark outside. Parking the car in the carpark Julie looked up at their window expecting to see the lounge light on; but she noticed their flat was in unusual darkness, which was extremely unusual as Mandy worked from home and always switched the lights on at the first signs of dusk. She would always be ready and waiting with a pot of tea for her. They would catch up on the day while drinking the brew, sometimes if Mandy wasn't too busy her sister would make up a batch of shortbread, which Julie loved.

But today all Julie returned home to was darkness and when switching on the light; in the lounge placed on the pale lemon Chesterfield coffee table had been a letter.

Jules,
 I decided to go on the adventure myself, thinking it would clear the air.
I'll be going to Duro, staying at The Gateway. I have left a text with Paul informing him too,
I'm hoping he will change his mind and miss me enough to join me there.
I'll phone you when I've arrived and booked a month away.
Enjoy work… lol.
             Mands x

TWO

With Mandy, there was no time like the present, that was for sure. Once she had made up her mind everything became a whirlwind and sometimes, Julie found it extremely exhausting. Mandy had indeed phoned her on The Gateway Pub phone telling her she had arrived and what a lovely place it was to relax with scenery and to see The Duro Rock from a distance. She said she would be catching the ferry and would be asking questions about their dad's family across the river.

Mandy had sounded excited but not too happy about there being no signal to use her mobile phone, but she said she could always drive the eighteen miles to the nearest town which she had been told would be the place to pick up the internet if needed, but this would work for now. Mandy had also let her know that the nearest village with a shop would be a few minutes by bus, and she'd also asked if she had heard from Paul. When Julie replied that she hadn't, Mandy was miffed about it.

Julie didn't hear from Mandy again for another two weeks. Obviously, she was very concerned and had tried Paul's phone number numerous times, but there was no answer. Julie also phoned The Gateway only to be told Mandy had checked out, her car still sat in the car park, and she had gone over to Duro Rock.

"She was returning," said the reply. "But no, they didn't know when."

Over the following few weeks Julie never heard from Mandy or Paul. She started to lose concentration at work and leapt for her phone every time it rang, but it was never them. She was frantic. Julie decided if she hadn't heard from either by the end of the week she would contact the police.

It was late afternoon when Julie heard from Mandy again. She was livid, it had brought up her anxiety levels, and Mandy had laughed at the other end of the phone when she told her this. Mandy told her she had caught the No:7 bus from the Gateway car park to take her into the village. On the journey, she noticed the beauty of the flat countryside with its rich colours and the scent which was released from the herbs as they were harvested.

Mandy met with the locals and mentioned to Julie how friendly they all were.

People from outside the village and in neighbouring towns would talk of witchcraft and Wicca doings at The Pastures. She was slightly perturbed to hear this but was determined to enjoy her adventure in Duro and she was also told Monica or Ma as the locals called her was still alive. Mandy sounded ecstatic and was hoping to meet their grandmother, Ma.

"Come and join me," she had pleaded. "There's so much to see and do."

In hindsight Julie wished she had taken Mandy up on her word, but she'd replied that she had taken on a new assignment at work. Julie picked up the irritation in her voice when she told her sister that she still hadn't heard from Paul.

"Neither have I," Mandy replied shortly. "His Loss!"
And that was the way she was.

There Julie would be worrying about someone, but not Mandy, if nobody had contacted her after a few weeks, she would brush them aside and move on.

The next telephone call Julie received from Mandy showed great excitement in her voice when she mentioned she'd met Monica, their grandma, 'Ma' as everyone called her. She lived on The Pastures on the other side of the River Duro on the opposite side of The Gateway Pub.
She lived off a track in a beautiful old cottage, which could be seen from Duro Rock.

Mandy said Ma was excited and happy when she had been introduced to her. There had been immense excitement in and around The Pastures upon her arrival. Ma had asked many questions about them. But never answered any questions about why she had put their dad up for adoption or if they had any other family. Mandy told Julie that she had been welcomed by Ma into her old farmhouse. She was led upstairs, the home was a huge eight-bedroom property with dark rooms, all décor was a mouldy yellow with low ceiling, pairing off from a long corridor which was aligned with brass effigies of face masks and headwear made from human hair, these masks were attached to dummies dressed in state regalia and were used for display, processionals, or commemorative ceremonies.
These figurines had frightened Mandy, she said Ma had just laughed and told her to stop being so silly.

The spacious landing overlooked the beautiful gardens had taken her mind away from the effigies and she had pushed her fear aside.

Mandy said when she was shown downstairs, there was a huge square room, rather like an old-fashioned pantry but on a much larger scale that Ma called The Freezer Room which contained chest and upright freezers which stood on a cold aged red quarry floor. Although Mandy said she wasn't shown inside the freezers, Ma had told her it was to slow down germination of plants. The certain ingredients used to make certain medicines had to be of a specific temperature.
Mandy said she had also noticed a raised wooden lid in the floor and had queried its place there.

"Ma, lifted the wooden lid," said Mandy excitedly. "And you will never believe what Jules?"
"Nope," Julie casually answered, but inside she was wishing she
 had been there too and felt slightly jealous.
"It was an old dried-up indoor well. There was also a room with several monitors for all the cameras placed around the farm's land to ensure no one would steal, tamper, or contaminate any of the agriculture." Mandy said she had also been shown around the vast array of spices, the crocus with their saffron, and the rows of orchids grown in the large polytunnels giving off their vanilla pods every nine months. The Echinacea or purple coneflower is also used in several forms, rich in antioxidants and to help with immunity. Some of the large polytunnels were home to berries to make cordials. There were vines with grapes hanging like jewels ready to be made into the finest of wines. Different types of nut trees, olive trees, and Sesamum Indicum with their pods full of sesame seeds growing to be made into oil or their seeds to be packaged to health shops. Rows of willow trees which Ma grew for their barks to make aspirin the old-fashioned way and the pale pink-headed Papaver poppy using the same technique but from the sap of the poppy heads to make pharmaceutical codeine.

There was a community of bee hives, and the collected golden-coloured honey was syphoned off and poured into glass jars of hexagonal shapes, the same as the prismatic cells of honeycomb found in beehives. Right at the end of the horticultural land was another track where tractors would pull the once-harvested produce to the different barns depending on their formatting to make the finished product.

There was one barn nearer to the house which had been modified and was surrounded by barbed wire. On one side growing up the wall were fast growing climbers: Russian Vine, Dogrose, Wisteria and Honeysuckle. Encircling the barn, just below its roof, were small windows. It was a strange looking building, and said she didn't notice an entrance. Ma had told her it had been designed to let in maximum natural light. Mandy had said she was told it was the pharmaceutical side, and nobody was allowed to enter unless you were authorised to work there, everything was top secret and vacuumed to a germ-free and sterile condition, and although Monica was involved in everything and had the last say, even she never entered the laboratory. Ma had also added that no animals were used in any of the pharmaceutical properties, she wanted everything kept as natural and to nature as the monks had managed to do centuries before when her forefathers had lived here and owned the land which had been passed through the generations.

"What I did find very strange though," said Mandy. All the staff were wearing long pale blue robes, and matching headscarves. It was quite creepy, no one spoke but they smiled and showed me around after being introduced as Ma's long-lost granddaughter."

Mandy went on to tell Julie that she'd also caught a ferry from The Gateway and taken the short journey to Duro Rock, she had explained at the time that because of the extreme rocks at the front of the island, all ferries had to journey around to the other side that faced the sea. It was unbelievably sandy on the other side, with a few gift shops and a shop selling local produce from their grandma's farm.

Across the harbour you could see the top of her seventeenth-century farmhouse, covered in ivy with its slanting roof.

Boats were coming in and out of the family inlet taking the finished products to meet the haulage ships further out to sea which took the products to their final destinations.

"Oh Julie, you should see the church and the hotel on The Rock. It's breathtaking. Inside the church are the most wondrous of paintings on the ceiling full of cherubs, the stained-glass windows when the sunlight hits them inside of the church lighting up like a spectrum of colours reflecting onto the walls. There are gold handrails at the end of the pews.

Inside the hotel is more like a mansion with its marble floors, and the decor with long velvet drapes. Its simplicity of grandeur can't be described."

She had gone on to say that when she had caught the local bus No:7 to the village shop and post office where she'd been given strange looks by a group of elders, they had said she looked extremely familiar and was sure they'd seen her somewhere before.

"I laughed," said Mandy, carrying on with the conversation, "I told them I was here meeting up with my grandma. But I do notice the locals are looking at me rather strangely."

"Maybe it's because you look so much like Monica, our grandmother?" Julie butted in.

"Maybe," Mandy replied. But she didn't sound convinced. She sounded slightly worried. "Anyway," she said quickly. "I must be off, I don't want to bore you. I'll phone you later."

More likely I was boring her, Julie thought. By the time she had asked her when she would be home and when she would phone next, Mandy had replaced the receiver.

Julie hadn't heard from Mandy for three weeks. She'd telephoned The Gateway again, but this time no-one had seen her or even knew where she was, but apparently her sister's car was still in the car park and hadn't been moved for the last two weeks. Julie was beginning to get angry about Mandy playing her cat and mouse games and worrying about her and where she was, why hadn't she phoned? By now Julie was out of her mind with worry and decided to report her as a missing person to the police.

At first, Julie wasn't sure in which area to report her sister as missing here where they lived or in Duro.

Neither the local police nor the police in Duro were interested when she had contacted them to report her sister as a missing person. Mandy was an adult and was quite erratic with her contact.

So, when Julie heard the knock at the door so late in the evening, thinking it was maybe Paul or Mandy, she called out their names and was extremely concerned about hearing the answer.

"It's the police," replied a woman's voice. Julie went cold.

Opening the door she met with a policewoman, a policeman both in full uniform, and a man who introduced himself as Clive, a detective.

Julie let them in and immediately felt nauseous. As they entered the flat, she noticed how observant the three of them were and how they absorbed the decor and style of the array. She felt uncomfortable and started to straighten the scatter cushions on the sofa.

"Here," she whispered, her throat dry, she could sense something dreadful was coming. "Take a seat."

"I expect you know why we're here," said the policewoman, who introduced herself as Mary.
"And" she added. "May I ask who Paul is?"

She pulled out a notebook, asking Julie to start at the beginning. As they took notes, they asked why she had reported her sister as missing.

Retelling the whole story from the beginning their eyebrows raised when she mentioned Paul, also adding she hadn't seen or heard from him since they had argued, and he had walked out.

The detective wanted to see a photograph of Paul and shuffled uneasily when he saw the photograph of him and Mandy together, both laughing at the camera. Clive passed the photograph to Mary and Tony, the policeman.

"Is everything ok?" Julie questioned, becoming more agitated by the minute.
But the police ignored her and carried on with their investigation. They told her they had gone to Duro and asked questions in the area. The police had impounded Mandy's car, and The Duro Police and forensic department

were checking it inside and out for any links to her disappearance.

On questioning the locals, Mandy had last been seen at the ferry side very close to the edge of the jetty looking into the waters and seeming to be in deep thought. Suicide had been speculated, although no suicide note had been found, the police could not rule it out, another theory was she may have just slipped off the jetty into the water and would never be found, what with the cold-water temperature and the strong tidal undercurrent. There wasn't a lot else that could be done, there was no evidence of foul play and everyone who had been questioned had mentioned she was a lovely lass with a great smile.

The investigators asked for Paul's address, but Julie didn't know it, so she gave them his phone number.

After a cup of tea, Clive suggested Julie see her GP for counselling and support and left her a contact card amongst other information and an investigation number. She could phone at any time, night or day.

Julie remembered Paul banging on her front door, angry that she had given the police his phone number. What the hell was she playing at? He said they had phoned him and had come to his house and had interrogated him.

"I haven't been able to contact you." Julie shouted.

He grimaced. "I've been under immense pressure at work. I'm as worried and concerned about Mandy, as you are," he said, as he swept his thick black hair back with two hands. As Julie looked at him, she noticed the concern on his face, but his look - it was almost like he knew something and was holding back.

THREE

It was almost morning when Julie eventually nodded off at The Gateway and awoke to the sun streaming through the thin pale green curtains that had seen better days. The fog had lifted outside and as she peered out of the window, the view she was confronted with took her breath away.

Mandy had been right about the beautiful scenery.

Directly below her were a few small boats moored bobbing gently on the river and although it looked like a millpond further out you could see a strong tidal undercurrent.

Across the riverside, she could see the wonderful colours of mauves, from the lavender, pinks of delicate petals of poppies, the different rows of coloured greens from different types of herbs and plants, the purple, and yellow-headed echinacea its different colours and varieties with its double or triple blossoms coming from humans self-pollinating the plants in labs and creating hybrids through vegetative propagation.

The tall looming sunflowers bowing their large golden heads, humble, towards the sun's rays. Breathing in the fresh air she leaned right out of the window as far as she could. To the right of her in the near distance was Duro Rock, the whole place was captivating, no wonder her sister didn't want to return home. Suicide was definitely out of the question, slipped into the water? Someone would have seen her for sure, it was a busy place.

Maybe Julie thought she was still here and had started a new life for herself.

Julie decided to shower, wash her hair, and put a little makeup on. She hadn't in months, and almost felt guilty in doing so, especially with her sister missing. It almost felt wrong, but she had to pull herself together for the both of them. Unfortunately, due to lack of water pressure, the shower was a waste of time and anything but relaxing.

Dressing casually in light cream utility trousers, a t-shirt and a white jacket with matching trainers, Julie slapped on some pale pink lipstick and grabbed her black Barbour crossover bag. She pulled the white bedsheets back to air the bedding. The Egyptian Cotton was luxury, at least that's something she supposed. She was ready for the day and was going to find out what happened to her sister one way or another.

As she came out of her room, she noticed how quiet the landing was, although there were only six doors, she had assumed the place would be fully booked considering its vicinity as the old rundown tavern was the only place to stay in and around the surrounding area.

Going down the stairs, Julie noticed there were no inviting photos or pictures on the walls, just a yellowing magnolia paint that had seen better days. Entering the door to the pub there was a bustle of people sitting around drinking coffee and eating breakfast, which surprisingly looked amazingly good.

The staff were polite and couldn't do enough for her.

Ordering a latte and full breakfast she went to sit outside. There were so many people and almost the same number of boats of all different sizes. A lot of the single manned boats were moored up directly outside The Gateway, and the larger boats were moored further up at the jetty by the car park, just as Mandy had described. Julie was certain she would be questioning everyone who came to view hoping someone surely would have seen her sister. She suddenly thought that maybe a lot of people here had seen Mandy but maybe they didn't know anything about her disappearance. Sipping her hot milky coffee, she thought how sad it was that they couldn't have shared this journey together.

It had also come to her attention that if she found out that something awful had happened to her sister then she could also face danger, who could she call? She had the police phone number but as there was no telephone signal nor internet, it meant she would be vulnerable, that was certain. Julie was letting her imagination run away with her. Poor Mandy, Julie hoped she would find her, maybe she would be at The Duro Rock. Julie could just imagine her now, sipping a chilled pinot, smiling, and saying.

"You took your time, didn't you?" as she flashed those blue doe eyes.

Her thoughts were interrupted by a shout.

"Ferry leaving in the next thirty minutes."

Julie thought she had better get a move on and hurriedly finished off the last piece of toast and mopped up her egg yolk with it.

"Best bit of the breakfast." Their dad had always said. She smiled, remembering him.

The sunshine was already warm, it was going to be a hot day. Julie was anxious as to what she might find. She felt unnerved as she made her way towards the car park. The gravel was dusty due to cars and mobile caravans arriving and leaving. She noticed there was a small campsite next to the car park with picnic benches and tents dotted around.

Although the area in general was flat, a few large willow trees sat along the riverbank giving a cool shade. The jetty itself was small with a sign which needed modernising 'SWIMMING or FISHING PROHIBITED'. She always wondered why signs like this were put up and couldn't understand why anyone would want to. The reeds, the river flow and the colour of the water would put anyone off.

As she stood in the queue of five waiting to catch one of the ferries to transport her over to Duro Rock. Julie wanted to look around for clues, even a piece of thread or anything of Mandy's. Maybe the police had missed something, but she was also afraid of looking too much because of what she might find. She wanted to look into the water. Maybe she would notice something lurking, but what if she did, and saw Mandy looking back at her under the water. Julie knew she was being silly and yet again overthinking, but she was also upset, emotional, and anxious.

Looking around the area, the hamlet looked so inviting and the ferrymen happy and helpful. Julie couldn't reason how Mandy could have vanished here.

She also noticed the car park was now full of all sizes of campervans and caravans - so that's where most of these tourists stayed, no wonder The Gateway's rooms were empty, but the restaurant was full.

Julie boarded the ferry and put her hand into her purse for Mandy's photograph. Surely at least one of the ferrymen would remember her striking looks.

"Yes, sure, I remember her," said the ferryman. "Lovely girl," He smiled a toothless smile. He had a warm and weathered look from working outside for so many years. "Yes," he repeated to himself. "The police were asking lots of questions, too. They checked all the boats along here; the sniffer dogs were in action, and they even had the divers out. Never saw that before."

"They were looking for my sister," Julie said quietly. "I'm visiting to see if I can shed any light on her disappearance, or even to find her."

"Oh," he replied, showing surprise. "You think she is alive? I hope you won't be too disappointed, as no one's seen her for months, we all presumed she drowned. Well." He paused. "That was the verdict anyway."

"Well," Julie replied. "I think the verdict is wrong."

With that, she turned her back and looked out towards the jagged-looking island as the ferry moved closer.

The bullrushes at the riverside and the marshes were left behind as the river forked into a delta, the water had changed from a millpond to slightly choppy and deeper.

The ferry took a right and swung out into the bay, finally revealing the wonder of the back of Duro Rock. The sight took her breath away, Mandy had been right with no exaggeration, the tiny island and view were indeed unforgettable. The sandy bay was like you would expect to find on a deserted Caribbean Island.

The hotel was stunning, a shimmering pink marble as the sun rays caught the building, which was next to a church, or she guessed one would call it an abbey.

The ferryman caught her attention.

"Would anyone like to take a photograph, before I moor up?"

The other passengers including Julie started taking photos and selfies with Duro Rock looming behind.

With expertise the ferryman steered the small boat to the moorings and helped with everyone's bags. Julie was the last one to disembark.

"Look," he said. "I'm sorry about your missing sister. Here," he smiled. "Take my card, I know there is no phone signal but if you ask for Jack with the ferry '*JACKIE*' the message will get back to me and I'll meet you either here for a lift back or at The Gateway for a coffee." He looked at Julie kindly. "Good luck with your search."

Julie was slightly disconcerted but thanked him and made her way to investigate Duro Rock.

She walked along a smooth pathway with a slight slope, a rope fencing on each side leading to some quaint small shops. About halfway up the rock, it was completely flat, as the path widened into a square full of coffee and wine bars. The bars had red and white striped awnings and silver round tables and chairs. The shops here at Duro Rock were laden with souvenirs of the monks from many years past, there were old black and white photos of The Gateway placed on the walls to buy, and postcards of the hotel and church were ample.

One of the larger shops caught Julie's eye, the perfumery grabbed her sense's. The shop was called *MA'S*.

Entering the store, it reminded Julie of a Victorian chemist, with its spit and sawdust floor and tinctures behind locked glass cabinets. On the black ashen countertop sat corked conical shaped bottles. A weighbridge was used to measure out different types of dried herbs, stored in an array of drawers.

She saw a young woman stock filling, who was extremely slight in build. Julie couldn't help noticing that she wore the same blue and white clothing that Mandy had mentioned Ma's workers wore over in the pastures.

Looking around everything sold there was from, and made on the farm, organic and naturally resourced. There were rows of golden honey in clear jars, beautiful small lace bags tied with a delicate bow that held herbs for different remedies. Rows of brown bottles with rubber-headed pipettes, each labelled and placed in alphabetical order covering all ailments, some of which Julie had never heard of.

"Oh wow!" She exclaimed. "All these potions and herbs for different ailments are incredible."

"Yes," nodded the girl who looked nervous as if she shouldn't be chatting. Her pale and withdrawn face looked so anxious. Julie expected people working and living here would be happy. She thought the whole area around Duro looked like Eden.

"I'm Julie," she smiled. "My grandma is Ma; I haven't introduced myself to her yet." She went on to tell her about her family and the disappearance of her sister Mandy.

Julie took the photograph from her purse and showed it to the girl, who inhaled sharply and slapped a white frail bony hand over her mouth.

"What?!" Julie said, startled. "Where's my sister? Do you know anything? Can you please help me?" She pleaded.

The girl looked so mouse-like and whispered as she looked around, furtively, "you are in grave danger. You must leave."

"Why?" Julie asked impatiently. "Where's my sister?"

The girl shrugged her shoulders. "That I don't know, but over the last few years, your sister and another girl who looked identical just vanished in this area; each one declared drowned, but no bodies had ever been recovered. Just go, please, for your own sake, just go." She begged, looking up at a security camera. "The Watchers are watching, and The Listeners are listening. They're always watching and listening."

She turned her back and started to serve someone else.

An elderly lady came over dressed in exactly the same attire.

"Do you want to go on your break now, Fiona? I'll cover for a while." looking over at Julie, quite disgruntled. "Yes?" She queried.

But Julie had gone. Entering the nearest coffee house and had a double shot of espresso.

What had happened here in this tranquil place, was Ma in trouble? Who was the other girl who went missing and proclaimed drowned?

Why was she in danger and asked to leave? Who were The Watchers and The Listeners?

Something about messages being sent on the breeze from the trees? Julie really wasn't sure. She felt pretty creeped out by it all, especially if her life was in danger.

Her head was spinning. She wasn't really sure what to do. Maybe Ma and her sister were both in danger. That notion gave her hope, but it also came with fear. She would try to find out more about this situation. If Mandy and Ma were in trouble it would be best if she stayed on this side of the river.

Mandy had sounded nervous on her last telephone call, and Julie was beginning to feel out of her depth. Mandy wasn't here on The Rock, but Julie needed to walk around the hotel and church and take a view from above to see if she could look over at Ma's farmhouse and land, just to familiarise herself with everything, just in case she was ever questioned about what she saw or heard here.

As Julie made her way up the meandering pathway she could look over to the right and see Ma's farm, from a distance she could see the endless polytunnels, greenhouses and the colours from the plants being cultivated, which was certainly a topic for local conversation. The barns loomed in the distance, and as Mandy had said the tallest barn surrounded by barbed wire was nearest to the farmhouse. The land seemed to reach out into the horizon.

To the left of her, she couldn't see much apart from manicured lawns surrounded by large almost tree-like pink and blue Rhododendrons. Turning the last bend of the path to the top of the rock, she reached the magnificent white marbled stone building, which looked pink against the sun's rays. The Duro Hotel. Its huge balcony windows, and the majestic large stone roaring lions on pillars as one walked towards the entrance of the building. The square grey stone plant holders alternated with Buxus pristinely shaped balls and hydrangeas, the large white mop-headed Macrophylla, the type of hydrangea chosen, was very apt for weddings. Someone certainly knew how to set the scene for wonder and glory.

Julie entered the palatial building, it was pleasantly cool and took away the harsh sun rays from her neck and head, all the tourists were wearing their sun hats or caps, unfortunately she'd left hers on the side of the bed at The Gateway.

She was confronted with a large reception area, a friendly-faced woman wearing matte red lipstick and nail polish to match, her whitened teeth showing off her perfect smile.

"Can I help?" She asked beaming.

Julie, feeling wary, after being told she was in danger, just replied, trying to sound casual.

"I'm just sightseeing," the woman nodded and answered a ringing telephone.

Julie walked along the off-white marble flooring which veered off three ways. In front was a huge library, almost museum-like. From the ceiling down were large books with dark brown spines, some of the books were open on a large round table and were written in Latin, and she thought others were written in Gaelic. In this large round room were a couple of pale blue chaise loungers with long blue velvet curtains fringed with dark blue pom poms finished off with scalloped pelmets. To the right was a cafe, with places of interest pamphlets placed on racks.

As she walked through to the left there was a ballroom, a dining room, and a bar that brought her out to a flat rolled lawn ending with a wide semi-circular enclosed wall made with rocks. A skep was still there, almost preserved in and around the rock where Monks had used these in their beekeeping times. The straw coiled basket turned upside down to create a cosy home for bees, with a small aperture located in the side for them to fly in and out. In the rock face was an arch with a statue of the Virgin Mary praying.

To the other side of the wall was a telescope view pointer, which took a £1 coin. Julie remembered how she and Mandy used to play eye spy with them when they visited the seaside and would race to the cliff tops to have the first go.

She inserted the coin and was surprised at how strong the magnifier was. As she swung the telescope to the right she could see over into Ma's land. The workers cultivating and cutting the fronds of plants into their woven baskets, she couldn't see their faces as they were being shielded by their blue headscarves.

Julie tilted the viewer down towards the jetty and the busy ferries on the River Duro. The Gateway pub was busy too. As she swung the telescope to the car park, she noticed a man standing there. It took her by surprise and sent a shock of hairs standing up on her neck. Surely not! The man she could see was or looked just like Paul, Mandy's boyfriend.

He was looking around; his hair was shorter, and he was clean-shaven but that was definitely his profile and stance.

Julie looked away for a second, then went back to double check but … the money had run out. She scrambled about in her large bag for her purse to find another one-pound coin. She noticed when putting the money for the second time into the slot, her hand was shaking. Looking into the viewfinder again the man in question wasn't there anymore. She doubted herself, perhaps it wasn't Paul, it had looked like him, or maybe it was because Julie wanted it to be him. She shivered. She decided to get back to The Gateway and lock herself in her room. She didn't want to explore. She felt unsafe and very alone and out of her depth. Mandy wasn't here, that was for sure.

Julie decided to catch the bus in the morning and visit the village to see if she could find out any information about her sister and try and find out who this other missing girl was. Then she would definitely be leaving this place.

What did that woman mean about The Watchers and The Listeners and why was she in danger? And who was the other girl that had gone missing years prior? No one, not even the police or detectives, had even brought up the other girl's disappearance. Julie's mind was in turmoil

FOUR

Julie was hoping as she made her way back to Duro Rocks' small sandy harbour that she would find Jack again, somehow, she felt she could trust him and ask him anything, she tried to stay cool and calm and act like everything was fine. But although she'd found nothing, her heart was still racing.

Julie had decided not to ask anyone else about her sister nor to tell anyone about Ma being her grandmother. Thank goodness she didn't resemble either of them.

Julie couldn't get down the pathway quickly enough and felt relief when she saw the small ferry *Jackie* moored up. Jack was there. Looking up, even from this distance he must have noticed the concern on her face.

"Hey?" he asked, frowning, as he helped her back onto his boat, "What's up? What happened up there? Are you ok?"

Julie explained about the woman who said she was in danger, and also told him she thought she had seen her sister's boyfriend Paul.

Then Julie asked Jack who are The Watchers and The Listeners.

He had simply answered. "They are the birds in the trees who send messages on the breeze."

"What?! Sorry? What on earth does that mean?" she cried out.

"It's always been like that here," he said. "It's basically gossip. As we have no mobile signal, messages are passed through people until it's delivered to the right person. I guess it's a bit like Chinese whispers."

Julie showed Jack the photo of her sister again.

"Please..., do you know what happened to my sister?" She asked sincerely and paused, he simply turned and started the engine.

Julie was left confused. They continued the journey back to The Gateway in an uncomfortable silence. As Julie was disembarking, she turned abruptly and said,

"Have you heard anything about the other girl that looked just like my sister who disappeared, apparently also drowned? It seems a very strange coincidence, don't you think?"

He surely must have heard something as he said he had worked on the river at The Gateway all his life, even as a boy he would come down to the jetty and watch and help as much as he was allowed.

He put his head down and averted his eyes away from hers.

He whispered back as if he was being heard or watched.

"I don't know what you are talking about." He hissed.

Julie walked away without saying another word.

She was hot and tired from the sun pelting down and noticed many people having drinks and food in the picnic area. She hurriedly made her way inside The Gateway.

She couldn't just accept that Mandy wasn't here and maybe, just maybe she had drowned. A nagging deep within had told her otherwise and she simply had to go with her gut feeling.

"Would you like a milky latte?" Asked the barman, "It looks like you could do with one, shall I bring it up to your room?"

Julie nodded, making her way upstairs, as her heart pounded, and her head raced. What on earth was going on here? She didn't want to stay and decided to pack and leave

after she'd caught the bus into the village the next day. She would call Clive and let him know she was here, and that she felt fearful, and had been told her life was in danger. She would also mention the other girl who had supposedly drowned here too, and that she was the image of Mandy.
Julie sat on the bed and looked out of the window, now feeling even more concerned about Mandy.

The barman knocked on the door with the latte and noticed her bag was already packed.

"Leaving already?" He asked in surprise. He was very young looking with short brown hair styled with a gelled flick at the front.
Julie nodded.

"Yes, sometime tomorrow. Something has come up." She answered, hoping she didn't sound nervous. But she was terrified.

"Here's your latte, enjoy." And with a smile, he handed Julie her coffee as he left and closed the door. Julie got up from the bed and locked the door after him.

The milky coffee tasted different, creamier with a very slight aftertaste which she couldn't quite make out.

She must have nodded off and when she awoke and had the most terrible headache her body felt shivery, almost hangover-like but worse.

Julie put it down to far too much sun from yesterday, she knew she should have worn a hat. And could hear her mother's voice now.

"C'mon Julie, put that hat on, the sun is stronger than you think, and you will catch it on the back of your neck, then you'll know about it." And this morning she certainly did.

Julie was still half dressed from the day before and didn't remember anything from sitting on the bed drinking her coffee
until now. Making her way to the bathroom to freshen up, she felt a bruise on the bottom of her heel and when looking, she noticed it was slightly red, raised, and very sore. Julie put it down to too much walking from yesterday. But

it was unusual though that the bruise was only on one heel and no other parts of her foot, just the bruise and no blisters. She winced when she put her weight on it.

Julie's head felt fuzzy, she felt so drained and tired, feeling perhaps she was going down with something.

It took Julie ages to get herself dressed; her limbs felt so heavy as if she was wearing ankle weights. What was happening to her?

Grabbing a couple of painkillers from her bag and downed them with a bottle of water she had in her bag from yesterday. Yuk!

It tasted warm too.

Julie gingerly made her way downstairs and into the bar, The Gateway was as busy as ever. To stay away from the bustle, she went to the other side of the bar, which was so much quieter and cooler, the large overhead fans were on a fast setting already; it was going to be another scorching day.

Looking around the tables there were board games, just the usual, chess, draughts and backgammon. Julie glanced at the bay window, and noticed a pathway, veering away from the side of the tavern. She waited at the bar to be served some fresh orange juice. Everything was pristinely clean, in complete contrast to upstairs. The optics, and so many types of gin, they were even selling local mead, the same bottles she had spotted in Ma's shop on Duro Rock. Julie couldn't believe it and moved closer for a better look. She noticed behind the bar was a piece of thread, a snagged thread from a jumper caught by a small splinter one may have thought nothing of. But to her, she knew exactly where it had come from, Mandy's tartan jumper. No one would have known it had come from that garment apart from her. It was a bright orange and blue tartan and every time she had worn it, Julie had asked her 'But why?' It was a ghastly coloured sweater which she had spotted in a charity shop and had fallen in love with it straight away.

Making sure there was nobody looking, Julie leaned across the bar and stretched over to the strand. Reaching over, she noticed the piece of thread had been caught above the latch door which she assumed led to the pub's cellar.

Julie held her treasured find, wrapping it securely into a serviette for safekeeping in her bag.

"Are you ok?" asked the bar boy. As he appeared from the other side of the bar, "Latte?"

"No thanks," Julie replied, curtly. She felt so rough she decided to have a fresh orange juice and bought a bottle of water and made her way towards the bus stop to catch the No7 bus into the village.

Julie's heel was bruised and extremely sore, she would have to go to the chemist and get some padding to help her walk better. She may even need a walking stick at this rate.

While sitting waiting for the bus, it saddened her as she looked at the area where Mandy had parked her car before it had been impounded.

Remembering when Mandy had first bought the red Peugeot 208.

"It's a GT as well, it goes pretty fast and holds the road well." Mandy had loved that car.

The bus was obviously running late, Julie supposed there wasn't much use for timetables around here. She decided to wander around to see if she could find any more clues but couldn't spot anything.

When it finally arrived, the bus was surprisingly busy.

The weather was slightly hotter than yesterday, but Julie still felt shivery and feverish. Stepping onto the bus, she asked to go to the village shop.

As soon as she arrived there, Julie would head to the telephone box and make her call to Clive, then she would be checking out and returning home and normality, that was for certain.

Sitting down, the bus driver had left the door open, and a fresh breeze wafted through the bus bringing a welcoming, refreshing relief to her clammy face. "That's beautiful," she thought, resting her head against the window.

Looking out, the whole surrounding area was flat with no hedgerows or trees, just endless areas of vegetation growing, mostly cabbages and cauliflower. Julie wondered what Mandy had thought when she had taken this same journey.

The jolting of the bus travelling along the small country roads made her feel nauseous. She was trying to take her thoughts away from feeling unwell. The bumpy journey wasn't helping matters. Julie reverted to thinking about her call to Clive.

She would mention she thought she had seen Paul, and whether the police had heard mention of The Watchers and The Listeners during their investigation. She couldn't get that thought out of her mind and was very perturbed by it. She had been told her life was in danger, obviously, that had totally unsettled Julie. Then, the other girl who had gone missing and the tartan thread. What was *that* all about?

Julie knew she needed to mention all these things, but her head still felt muddled and hazy, she kept losing her concentration. Not dreaming, just drowsing.

The bruise on her heel was enlarging too and she was struggling to put any weight onto it. She knew something had to be going on here, but what was it? This wasn't the Julie she knew.

Julie felt like she'd been sitting on the bus all day, still seeing nothing much of anything. The scenery hadn't changed. There were no high rises, shops, garages, or even pubs, all the things she was used to. It felt like she had simply missed a hundred years, and that she had somehow fallen into the last century, and time had just stood still. Even in her current state, Julie knew this was an irrational thought, and totally out of character.

The road was winding with side roads meandering off, you could see that one could easily get lost if you didn't know the way. A thought, only a small, but hopeful thought suddenly popped into her head. Maybe Mandy had lost her way and was out here in the fields? Nonsense. Now *that* was ridiculous thinking. Even in her confused state she knew it.

A small, thatched house came into view Julie realised it was indeed the shop with a post office, the old-fashioned red pillar telephone box outside. A group of elderly women were chatting next to the shop window, who stopped in their tracks as she approached.

Still feeling unnerved, Julie smiled as she said "Hello." No one replied as she entered the shop.

The woman behind the counter fitted Mandy's description of her perfectly. So, Julie knew this woman had met her sister. Taking a deep breath, Julie took out Mandy's photo.

"Good God!" Exclaimed the wrinkle-faced lady.

"Yes?" Julie questioned.

"Um," The shopkeeper paused. "Actually, I'm not sure." Looking at Julie's face she carried on saying for her to wait here, and she would be back.

Going outside she looked around, almost on edge to check there was no one around who shouldn't be.

"Quick!" she called to the small crowd. "In here now."

The gossiping females entered the shop and eyed Julie with suspicion who was still holding Mandy's photograph.

"I know you have met my sister," Julie said. "She told me she had been here and described you to me."

Waiting with bated breath for the answer to her next question.
"Does anyone know anything about what happened to her? Or anything that could help me find her, I'm desperate."

One lady, slightly older very smartly dressed wearing a hat answered her saying,

"Which girl are you asking about?" She stopped talking abruptly. And looked around at the other women as if to ask permission. She carried on nodding, "as there was another girl who also looked the same as the one in your photograph who also went missing and also came here looking for her family and lost Grandma."

"What happened?" Julie asked, still feeling seriously under the weather with a stomping headache. She stumbled, almost crippled with exhaustion and the feeling of nausea still looming, needing to sit down. The lady behind the counter brought over a chair for her to sit on.

Julie heard someone say, "I think she is going to faint." Dizziness crept over her.

Julie passed out. When she came round, she was in a lovely freshly laundered bed, a warm soft breeze filtering through beautifully measured to made white cotton curtains, fringed with the tiniest of pink rosebud print. There was a white Victorian jug and bowl next to an old, faded pine bedside cabinet.

She sat up bolt right with a splitting headache and a massive bandage wrapped around her ankle under her foot as protection for her heel, she could smell something surgical.

Where the hell was she? panicking she had the animal instinct to get out of there right now. Putting her feet onto the floor, a hard varnished pine.

Still feeling dizzy and trying to stand, Julie somehow limped as she made her way to the large wooden, white-painted door with a black painted latch. The floorboards creaked underneath as her feet made their way to what she hoped would be her escape route. It was locked.

Julie sat back on the bed and cried. She was thankful that nobody had undressed her, so she checked to see if her money and phone were still in her bag. Nothing had been touched.

It took her a few moments to struggle back into the comfortable bed. The exhaustion washed over her again and her limbs felt so heavy that she just gave into the weariness and drifted in and out of sleep, not knowing or caring anymore where she was, the day, time or even what would happen to her.

Julie had finally given up.

FIVE

When Julie woke up, she was still in the same peaceful bedroom, but as she came to, she knew she wasn't alone, and that someone else was in the room with her.

Turning her head there was a chair in the corner which she hadn't noticed before. Paul was sitting there, but it couldn't be him, could it? It must be a dream.

"Julie are you ok?" she heard him ask. She was definitely dreaming. Why would Paul be here? Confusion added to her thoughts, only just coming round, after a strange night's sleep.

"Paul, is it really you?" She asked with doubt. He stood up and came towards her.

"I'm so glad you are ok." He smiled as he sat at the bottom of the bed. He asked, sounding sincere, but although she knew him, she still didn't know enough about him to be sure. Julie was a good judge of character. The sentiment was in his eyes, but behind his question was nothing. He really didn't care, and clearly had no real interest in her answer.

Julie nodded but was still not sure of exactly what was going on. And that was what she wanted so badly. To understand, so she could start to get her head around everything. Why she constantly felt so nauseous and dizzy. And why did her heel still hurt so much?

"I guess I've got a lot of explaining to do." He said sheepishly. Paul sat at the end of the bed and apologised again. "Maybe I should start at the beginning."

"No! Don't start at the beginning!" She said sharply, not recognising the tone in her voice. She was frightened and confused, but above all she was angry. Really angry, her mind was raging.

"Why don't you start with the here and now? Maybe with the truth, and something I can understand. I have no idea where I am and why you are here? I have absolutely no idea who or what you really are. I don't really know you. All I know is that Mandy was besotted. To me, you are just Mandy's ex-boyfriend, who suddenly disappeared, wanting nothing to do with her plans. And that tells me something. It tells me something about you. I'm not sure that's good."

Julie was trying to sound strong but felt anything but. She'd always considered herself a strong person but had never felt this vulnerable. Being kept prisoner, locked in a strange house with her missing sister's ex-boyfriend, and with no mobile signal, and no way to contact the outside world. She was totally lost, completely out of her depth. All the hope in her was gone. She'd lost everything. She still didn't know what was going on. Maybe she could lose her life too.

Paul started talking immediately. He told her that his aunt owned and ran the village shop, and he was an undercover detective. Julie was very dubious. From what little she knew about him, she couldn't help it.

He went on, saying that a few years previously another young woman, about Mandy's age had also supposedly drowned at the jetty. Everyone had accepted this, seemingly without question. But when he had decided to look further into it, things just didn't ring true. He just didn't think he could walk away. With his aunty hearing bits of hearsay, he'd decided to stay here in Duro, working undercover to try to find out anything about the girl who had disappeared. Her name was Susan Miles.

He'd found out that her mother, who had been adopted, had also died from a rare blood disorder when Susan was young. She had traced her family tree back to the village. It turned out Ma was her grandmother.

"Oh wow!" Julie gasped. This news was almost unbelievable.

He nodded. "She was the exact image of Mandy. So, when I saw you two at that club, I thought I was seeing Susan. It threw me completely."

Julie still wasn't sure if she believed him. She wanted to, but just couldn't take that last leap of faith. But what he'd said sounded pretty convincing, and she guessed it made sense.

"It opened the case up again for me, and when you and Mands started talking about your father, who had been adopted and had also passed away from a rare genetic blood condition and the family was traced back here, I needed to find out as much as I could."

Julie interrupted him, with a voice she didn't recognise, and with so much venom said. "So, you just used Mandy for information to help you with this Susan girl case?"

Paul dropped his head, resignedly, then looked directly at her. The discomfort was clear on his face. Good, Julie thought, face up to what you have or haven't done. She had no sympathy for this person in front of her. She thought of herself as a fairly decent person, but just couldn't find it in her heart.

"At first, yes. But then I fell in love with your sister, not expecting I would, but then, I'm sure I don't know how love works, but then, does anyone? When Mandy suggested we all visit Duro and get married at The Rock. At one point, I probably would have. Then, thinking logically, I knew I would have blown my cover, especially coming here to the village of my family with a girl the image of Susan also related to Ma." He took a deep breath and looked at Julie. "Did you get a chance to visit Ma's? Have you met your grandma yet?" He raised his eyebrows, waiting for a reply.

"No," Julie replied. After what she'd seen and been going through this she wondered if this might put Ma in danger. "Listen, Paul, I have no idea what is going on here, why I'm locked in this room. Why are my dreams so indistinct and incoherent? You know..., I know you know."

Looking at her questioningly, his face looked more lined and tired than she remembered it. He said nothing.

"It was that woman on Duro Rock. She looked scared and said I was in danger and told me about The Watchers and The Listeners...I'm absolutely terrified, Paul." Julie said.

"And I don't care what people say, I know with complete certainty that Mandy never fell off that jetty or would attempt suicide, that's not her. You must have seen what sort of person she is? Surely? I just want to know where she is. Do you think it's possible she is being held against her will?"

Paul never answered, he was infuriatingly good at that. He just nodded and kept holding her hand, looking at the floor. Could Julie really trust him? She so wanted to, she badly needed a friend, but still didn't know if he was the 'friend' she was looking for.

Without another word, Paul got up and left, locking the door behind him. As he left, she told him she just wanted to go home. As she heard him walking away, she heard him say, almost as an afterthought, that she would be safer here than anywhere else. It didn't help, it didn't calm her, it wasn't at all reassuring. Despite the explanations, or just telling her what he thought she needed to know to keep her quiet, she was still a prisoner.

An elderly woman walked in, introducing herself simply as 'Aunty', and brought Julie a tray of sandwiches, egg and cress, and salmon and cucumber in thinly cut white bread. She came across as a motherly character slightly stout wearing a housecoat and apron. She bustled about the room anxiously.

"How are you feeling now, Dear?" She asked with sincerity, it almost sounded like she meant it. "Did Paul tell you that you had been drugged at The Gateway? That's why you were feeling the way you were when you fainted."

Julie didn't reply. She didn't really know what to say. Drugged, she thought? Why? This was not what she had expected. She had no answer to the question. Why had Aunty said that? He hadn't mentioned anything to her about her being drugged, when he was 'explaining' what was going on.

Julie thought back to when she had blacked out, her memory still jumbled and disjointed, when she tried to put thoughts together. She remembered starting to feel woozy and foggy headed when she woke up at The Gateway. She'd blamed the way she was feeling on too much sun at The Rock. She remembered that evening drinking a latte which had been brought to her by the friendly young barman she had met at breakfast. The drink had left a strange aftertaste.

Julie mentioned it to 'Aunty' as Paul had said to call her that. She really wasn't sure if she should have said anything about the weird-tasting latte at The Gateway, as Aunty turned around quickly and looked at her, almost sternly.

"Did you tell Paul?" She asked. "Did you tell him that your latte tasted strange?"

Julie shook her head. "No," she replied. "But…, are you certain I was drugged?"

Aunty looked at her for a long time, but never answered.

"Is there anything else you need?" She asked, all the motherliness suddenly gone.

Shrugging her shoulders, Julie replied that she'd just like to go home, and if she wasn't being held prisoner, as she was repeatedly being told, why wasn't she allowed to use the telephone to talk to the detective who was following her sister's case.

"I still have his card," she mentioned eagerly.

Aunty tutted, sounding almost exasperated, almost like she was answering a question from a young child.

"Oh no, no, Dear!" She exclaimed, chuckling like Julie had asked the stupidest thing ever. "Now that would bring no good to anyone. You are safe here and I will look after you. While Paul is looking for evidence and you are here, all will be well." She smiled, "do you like to read, Dear?" She asked kindly.

Not really understanding what Aunty was saying, Julie meekly nodded. Now she wasn't feeling so disorientated, she needed some sort of brain exercise. There wasn't even a television to watch. But whatever was going on here, she knew she had to find a way to get out. Despite what she was being told, this didn't feel like this was protection, it felt like imprisonment.

"Aunty?" she asked, which still seemed a strange thing to call her, as she was a complete stranger to her. "Do you really believe I was drugged? And if so, do you know why? And by who? I'm only visiting, looking for my sister." Julie felt tears start to well up in her eyes but was determined not to cry.

Again, Aunty didn't reply, but as she walked out, she turned to look at Julie. "Best to ask Paul about those things," she said, enigmatically. She left, locking the door behind her.

The attempted conversation with Aunty had left her frustrated, and angry. She genuinely seemed to have her best interests at heart, but she'd really answered nothing. Drugged? By whom, and why? Maybe the same thing had happened to Mandy, but, again, why? She wasn't even sure how long she'd been in this room since passing out in the shop.

Perhaps people were being drugged at The Gateway and then unwillingly taken somewhere? But, if that was the case, who could possibly be behind this?

With so many visitors in and around the area, this would surely have come to the attention of someone here. Julie's mind unwillingly went into overdrive. What if the villagers were all involved in something sinister? It was unthinkable although she knew it had been known in extremely rural areas. Julie tried not to think about it.

This was something she didn't believe in and couldn't accept. Her mind simply refused the thought.

Julie hoped back home her disappearance had been noticed and someone had reported her missing, but, more than that Clive was looking for her.

Aunty returned with a cup of tea. Somehow, Julie needed aunty to trust her, to let her think she was happy here and wanted to stay, maybe she wouldn't keep her locked up if the trust was there.

"So?" Julie asked casually, sipping at the scalding tea, which was very sweet, (almost too sweet) and served in a matching rose patterned bone China cup and saucer set. "When is Paul coming back?"

Aunty looked up in the air and sighed theatrically. "Who knows, dear," She replied. "All I know is I have to look after you and keep you safe."

Julie asked her about the village, and if she had been born here. She replied to how different life had been in those days. "I'm almost ninety years old."

"You certainly don't look it," she butted in, without thinking.

"Well, my Dear," she replied, smiling, "that's a very nice thing for you to say. In fact, I've always used Ma's products," and she beamed at her with her intense blue eyes, and what Julie thought was a real smile. In that smile she could certainly see the uncanny resemblance between her and Paul.

"As I was saying," she carried on, looking out of the window, her memories obviously taking her back to earlier years. Aunty wasn't really here anymore, well, not in the room.

Mandy would have taken advantage of this situation and probably have pushed the elderly lady out of the way and escaped. Julie couldn't do a thing like that, but she needed to find a way to get to the telephone.

Paul's aunt told her she had been born here in this building, and her family had had this shop and Post office for well over one hundred years.

There had been farming at Duro as far back as the eighteenth century and monks had dwelled on Duro Rock well before the fourteenth century. They had kept bees, making honey and mead, which in time was sold locally and far afield. The monks had grown herbs, making natural potions and people would travel along the River Duro to visit and have their ailments cured, handing over silver and gold in return for a healing cure.

"It sounds fascinating," Julie said. Aunty smiled, enjoying the chat and attention.

"It made the monks and the area very profitable. I was also at school with your Ma." She went on to say.

"My Grandma?!" Julie stuttered. "You know Ma?"

'Yes of course, dear, we grew up together here in the village."

Julie really didn't like to keep being called 'Dear'. It made her feel like an infant, someone not to be taken seriously. Even in her current state, it was infuriating.

"Please, can you call me Julie?" she interrupted.

"Yes, dear", said Aunty as she carried on reminiscing, obviously not having listened, or heard a word she'd said.

"Your Ma and Pa were at the same school as me, we were quite friendly." Julie knew this was something she needed to listen to. It might actually be the key to help her escape from whatever this was. But escape had gone from her mind for the time being. She just needed to survive whatever this was, and she needed to know about her grandparents and this woman, Paul's Aunty may let something slip which might help to solve the mystery of her sister's disappearance.

Aunty told her that Ma's family owned The Pastures.

What took Julie by surprise was when she mentioned that Pa's family had owned The Gateway in the last century. It had once been used as a coaching house, where locals would store their produce and in turn use their boats as transport up and down the river to sell and barter.

"Your Pa's parents were second cousins who had married each other, and so had their parents. This was becoming quite confusing, but it was very common here in the hamlet for cousins marrying cousins and second cousins, being only a few of us children in the adjoining villages, and all the same sort of age.

They fell in love quickly and were married by the time they were sixteen. You could almost say it was love at first sight." She seemed to smile to herself, paused for a while, and with a totally empty, emotionless stare, she said, "I never saw your Pa ever again."

Julie wanted Aunty to carry on talking about her family and Duro, but then the front doorbell rang.

Paul's voice called up.

"It's me. How are we all?"

"All's well Paul." Replied his aunt. Julie wanted to tell him all was most definitely not well!

He entered the room, smiling, Julie noticed the floorboard creak, it was the nearest part by the door entrance. She knew if she was ever getting out of here, that floorboard must be avoided.

When she eventually got away from here? She was desperate to find that telephone, she knew it was here somewhere upstairs and must be close as she had heard it ring a few times. But where?

Paul beamed at her but seemed to only be speaking to Aunty. As if she wasn't even there.

"Well, I've been to Duro Rock and The Gateway to see if I could pick up anything, but everything seems to be settled." Aunty smiled and nodded.

Looking directly at Julie, Paul, but with no warmth said,

"Aunty told me that you love to read, come with me and choose some books from the library."

Julie followed him limping across a square landing with two doors, and a long corridor heading off to what could only be another wing in the old building. The stairs were on the right, Julie tried to take in her bearings to plan an escape route.

The room was square and smelt musty with three walls filled with books from floor to ceiling. Some were so old and written in Gaelic and olde English.

"I don't know where to start," Julie said.
Paul held up a carrier bag.

"Take what you want, you can always get more when you've finished these." Again, he smiled at her reassuringly.

Julie asked Paul how long and why she was being held captive, but the question fell on deaf ears. He just ignored her.

A telephone caught her eye amongst the fourth wall of files and paperwork as she was looking through all the books, so there it was.

Julie's heart leapt, she needed to escape from the bedroom she was imprisoned in, and somehow make it into Aunt's library to use the phone and call Clive.

She would have to make sure Paul wasn't in and Aunty would be behind the counter serving in the shop. She selected a few books, and Paul added a few more, putting them into the bag. Julie shuffled her way back across the landing to her room.

Not another word was spoken by either of them. As soon as she had returned to the confines of her bedroom, Paul and Aunty both left, locking the door behind them.

Julie couldn't get her head around why Paul's Aunt hadn't seen her grandad since he had married Ma, and what about this news that his family had owned The Gateway?

Julie still hadn't found out who or what The Watchers and The Listeners were, but one thing was for sure, she was going to get out of here.

She opened the bag of books left at the foot of the bed for her to read, there were so many different genres. Paul had added to the bag as she was sifting through Aunty's library. Magazines, and novels written in the early seventies,

gardening books, and   local points of historical interest. How long did they want to keep her here as a prisoner? Julie thought.
Paul hung around for a few days, she could hear him talking and often laughing with his aunt but was never able to pick up their specific conversations.

In the mornings she was brought toast and honey (from Ma's thriving bees). Some sort of stew at lunchtime, scones and sandwiches for tea and always a hot milky drink with two biscuits.

"You don't need to worry about anything Dear, the time will pass soon enough. Just read the books and they can always be replaced by more when you've finished."

Looking out of the window, to one side were the marshes, and on the other, there were fields as far as the eye could see. Even shouting at the top of her lungs would make no difference, there was nobody around to hear. Julie guessed that the room she was in was farthest away from the shop downstairs. She may even be in a room that was part of an unseen annexe, she couldn't be certain.

She *had* to find a way to that telephone, and somehow knew they were planning to do something with her, she needed to get out of here, as soon as possible.

Early one evening, Julie heard Paul call out from the hallway to Aunty he would be leaving for a few days and Jack would be calling in just to check all was still ok and going to plan. So, Jack, the man from the jetty who took her to The Rock, was also involved in whatever was going on here.

Julie heard Paul coming upstairs and the creak and unlocking of the door. He popped his head around.

"Just checking if you are, ok?" He asked. "I have to go away for a few days. Please behave for Aunty." And that was it.

Before Julie could say anything or ask any questions, he'd relocked the door, and she heard his footsteps going down the stairs. She was absolutely furious.

He called out to Aunty, "Yep, all's well, I'll see you in a few days." The front door closed, and she heard the roar of his car pull away from the village.

Julie's heart raced. Now was the time.

She remembered watching a film where someone was trapped, in a locked room who had escaped by placing some paper under the door of the room they were in and with a hair grip, they wriggled the lock until the key had dropped, which they then pulled towards them, bringing them the key. Ripping a page from one of the old magazines, taken from Aunty's library, she rummaged around in the bedroom until she came across a few Kirby pins. What were the chances? These days they are just called hair grips. More to the point why, now, in this situation did she remember that? She didn't really care, as long as they still did the job.

"Luck, please be on my side." She pleaded, although she didn't really believe in that type of thing. She was ready to take any help she could get.

She slipped the sheet of paper under the door, placed the Kirby grip into the key lock and began to jiggle the wire. It was a lot harder than it looked in the films and wasn't working. Her heart began to race, and palms to sweat. What would Aunty do if she caught her? Aunty had said that she was here to look after her, and keep her safe, but what had she been told to do to her if she didn't behave as 'they' wanted? She frantically scrambled around in her bag for something else that would help with the escape. Maybe a metal nail file would work? Mands had always told her to change to a natural emery board. But this time Julie was pleased she had got her own way.

Holding the file at the bottom of the lock and juggling the grip at the top, Julie soon heard the soft thud on the paper, as she carefully pulled it towards her the key was sat in the middle. Julie smiled triumphantly, come on girl you've got this, she said to herself.

Quickly, carefully opening the large heavy door, she remembered to walk into the hall avoiding the creaking floorboard that she always heard when someone was entering what she simply now considered a cell, and personal hell. Her heel was still agony, but the pain was manageable. She was at a stage when she really didn't care. Julie was determined to get to the telephone and make this call.

She could hear muffled voices from one of the rooms downstairs.

She was anxious and she was absolutely terrified. Her mouth was dry, and she was sure that someone must be able to hear her panicking heart beating. So loud and fast. With sweating palms, she gingerly crept her way across the landing, which was dimly lit, casting shadows on the large wooden floorboards. The shadows in the corners made her shudder. Summoning up visions and unwanted thoughts about The Watchers and The Listeners., whom she still had no real idea about. Who or what were they? Just the name scared her.

Aunty's library door was open, and she could see the phone. Her pounding heart was deafening in her ears. She reached into her pocket for Clive's card, then realised she had left it in her bag. Julie's stomach just dropped.

"How stupid," She thought. "Mandy would certainly have given her a good telling off for that one."

She heard someone coming upstairs and panicked. She wanted to curl up or even give herself in. Her mind couldn't absorb what was happening. Her brain was already fragile, her head was spinning out of control in fear. The fight or flight reflex kicked in. Could she simply pretend that she was getting more books? But then she'd need to explain how she'd managed to get out of the room in the first place. And she didn't know how to.

"Hold on." She heard Paul say. Julie heard him going back downstairs. "Are you ok, Aunty?"

She let out a huge sigh of relief. The adrenalin rush left her breathless. Gathering herself, she slowly started to tiptoe back to her 'cell' She hadn't even heard Paul return. But then, she'd had other things on her mind.

She then realised that what she was trying to achieve was such a stupid idea. It was all very well playing Houdini and escaping from the locked room, but now she was back, exactly where she'd started, and still no closer to the phone. How could she re-lock the door from the inside? She couldn't, there was no way. She inserted the key into the lock, gently closed the door, and sat back on the bed, knowing that she had no choice but to see how this was going to play out.

Outside the door, Julie heard the key try to turn, but of course, it was already unlocked. She heard Paul fervently muttering to his aunt. Her stomach churned, and she felt sick.

"You must make sure you lock the door behind you." He tried to whisper, unsuccessfully. "You know it's for her own good, and the only thing that's going to keep her safe."

Paul's Aunt opened the door and smiled at her. It was a kindly smile, but totally empty of feeling or comfort. It was just an act, a façade, and not a very good one.

"Would you like anything to eat or drink?" She asked.

Julie replied with a brisk shake of her head, then asked bluntly, "How long are you planning on keeping me here? I need to get back home for work; to pay bills, and my friends will be worried about me, and I'm pretty sure I'll be reported as a missing person." Julie looked at her straight in the face, looking for answers.

Aunty just smiled serenely, saying that she was sure that Paul had everything in hand and under control, and there was nothing for her to worry about, besides she added, "You are safe here with us."

But from who exactly, she thought? So she asked, "But safe from who?' Who am I supposed to be afraid of, and why? I only came here to try and find out what happened to my sister."

"We just must always be on our guard." she replied, looking straight back, but through her. "But I will speak to Paul."

Aunty left without further discussion. The door was locked again. She heard them going back downstairs. Another muffled conversation. Her heart was beating so hard and fast, and after her failure to make that phone call, she didn't have the presence of mind to try and listen to what they were saying. Julie was done.

She heard Paul shout "Good-bye." Then the car roared off for the second time. She wasn't sorry to hear him leave. He confused her, and she was already far beyond confused.

The following morning, she was still half asleep when Aunty brought in breakfast. She cleared her throat and placed the tray of food next to her.

"Morning Dear," Aunty beamed as Julie opened her eyes, and slowly sat up. She was getting to hate that smug, false smile. It was all an act, she thought to herself.
She doesn't care about me; she is simply following orders, thought Julie but from whom, or why, she still couldn't fathom.

"Here's your toast and honey, and as you refused your drink last night, I've made you a nice pot of tea." Aunty lifted the bone China teapot and poured Julie a cup. "If you don't mind, I think I'll join you this morning," she said, filling herself a cup. Julie was taken aback, this was something Aunty had never done before. But although in some way she welcomed the company, she couldn't fully relax because she was still so suspicious about what was going on here.

"How come you never saw my grandpa after he got married?" Julie blurted out. "And does my family still own The Gateway?"
It had been going over in her mind what she had been told until Paul had rudely stopped their conversation when his aunt was discussing to Julie about her family. She needed to know so much more, and who were The Watchers and The

Listeners? Jack had said they were found in the trees and carried on the breeze, or words to that effect.

Aunty leaned in towards her, almost nervously, and her voice dropped to a whisper. "You see, Dear, your Pa had been born with the golden blood. They say it is the blood of the Gods." Julie laughed out loud.

"Does that make him immortal?" she said, not believing a word of what this woman had just said to her. But, for once, the sincerity in her eyes told Julie otherwise. Aunty left her tea and without another word walked out, locking the door. As always.

SIX

Julie drifted in and out of sleep most of the day and didn't remember finishing breakfast or Aunty coming in and collecting her tray.

The next few days and nights rolled into one, and Julie totally lost track of time. Food and drinks were brought up to her seemingly at random times.

"C'mon Dear." she would hear Aunty say. "That's it, eat and drink it all up, I've made everything especially for you. You need to keep your strength up."

Julie woke early and the sun was just rising, although she felt a little groggy a thought arose. Was she being drugged? Nothing seemed to make sense anymore. Her mind and thoughts were beginning to jumble, making scrambled words and images go around in her head.

She could hear loud voices downstairs and distinctly heard Jack's voice.

"Are you sure this is going to work?" He was asking.

"I hope so." Was Paul's reply. "We can't keep her here much longer, there are too many questions, and rumours are starting to spread around the village.

"I'll pop upstairs and see her in a while, I'm sure once she hears the plan, she will think it would be a good idea."
Julie heard Aunty interrupt. "I don't think she truly trusts us. I've been adding valerian into her drinks, only a little just

to keep her sleepy, I wouldn't want The Watchers and The Listeners to pick up on anything."

What on earth were they planning? Julie had to find out. It had even entered her mind that her sister was being held here in one of the bedrooms. Either way, Paul and his aunt were definitely involved in her disappearance that she was sure, and Jack knew about it too. She was being drugged with valerian to make her feel drowsy and disorintated. Julie wondered how long she had been here, locked in this room.

Julie heard footsteps coming up the stairs. She could feel a surge of rage which she had never felt before, her fear had turned into anger.

Paul entered smiling, carrying a tray, balanced with a cup of tea, a matching plate of toast and honey, and a bag.

"Morning," he smiled, his dimples as prominent as ever. "So glad you are awake early. I've come up with a plan."

Julie launched herself towards a startled Paul pushing the tray along with its contents over him.

"Go away!" she screamed. "Leave me alone!"

Her voice had so much venom behind it. Her throat was dry, and she could feel hot tears of frustration streaming down her face.

"You made out you were my friend, and you were helping me, and I began to trust and believe you, but you let your stupid weird Aunt drug me constantly with valerian, feeding me lies about my grandpa being born with blood from the gods? I've never heard such rubbish! And who are these stupid Watchers and Listeners?

Oh My God!" Julie started to shake, "I think you are behind my sister's disappearance."

Paul dropped the tray, holding her wrists and pushing her back onto the bed, and through gritted teeth whispered. "Now you listen to me, Julie, my Aunty and I have welcomed you here, we have made you safe and jeopardised our safety. And," he added, "I swear I have no idea what has happened to your sister."

He slowly loosened his grip and used the bed sheet to mop up the mixture of tea, butter, and honey from his face.

"Is everything alright in there, Love?" called out his aunt opening the door with Jack following close behind.

"Uh oh," laughed Jack, looking at the mess of breakfast remains. "Julie didn't like your idea then?" He laughed, "or was it just the breakfast?" He seemed to find it hilarious.

Paul didn't answer. Julie could sense the anger coming from him, and so could Aunt and Jack.

"I haven't had a chance to tell her about it yet," Paul replied, still glaring at her. "In fact," he said, looking directly into Julie's eyes. "After her little outburst, I don't think I'm going to help her anymore."

The room went silent. Paul stormed out, while the other two exchanged looks of despair, then both looked at Julie for answers.

"What?" Julie shouted vehemently. pushing off the food-ridden bedsheet. Her anger had given her a release of adrenaline and she didn't care anymore about anything.

"Seriously," she laughed sarcastically. "You keep saying you are helping me, but you keep drugging me and feeding me with lies."

"No, we aren't, Dear," replied Aunty. "A little valerian doesn't hurt anybody."

Paul came back into the room, banging the door behind him. He had changed into a black tracksuit. Sitting down and taking a deep breath, as if hoping to calm matters down.

"Look Julie," he said, but quietly, "You can believe whatever you like, but on a very serious matter, The Watchers and The Listeners have been spotted around here, and villagers are talking and speculating. Although no one knows for certain that you're staying here, if villagers find out it may put Aunty and you in danger."

Shrugging her shoulders Julie replied bluntly, "so, what idea do you have?" Jack looked down at his feet and Aunty became fidgety, which Julie noticed she did when her anxiety levels rose.

"We have decided it's for the best if I drive you back home."

Julie leapt at Paul's words. He carried on, explaining that there was too much gossip going on in the village. He had already picked up her bag from The Gateway just after she had collapsed here at his Aunty's Post office. He had put it in his bedroom for safe keeping. Then he said he had put the word out there that she had caught the train home.

"But then we had that detective Clive turn up, snooping around asking questions."

Good Julie thought to herself, things were looking up with Clive and his team now involved again. Hopefully, work or even her neighbour, Angela could have reported her missing. Angela knew she didn't like to stay away from home for long and her holidays were always short and sweet. Julie was also glad she had informed all of her and her sister's friends along with their work buddies where she was going and where she would be staying. As she hadn't been able to contact anyone since her arrival, they had become concerned and suspicious, especially as Mandy had gone missing. Thank God for neighbourly Prosecco nights and girly catch ups.

Julie saw Paul pick up the paper bag he had brought in on the breakfast tray from earlier. Reaching inside he pulled out a box of dark brown hair dye.

"Here," he nodded, handing it to her. "Aunty will cut and colour your hair like Jack's." He couldn't be serious, could he? But looking at his face she realised he was.

"It will be easier this way. Jack has moored up *Jackie* and informed The Gateway he is going to Wales with me for a holiday."

"Don't worry, Dear," butted in Aunty, "it will be ok, you'll see." She must have seen the fearful expression on Julie's face. "Jack will keep his head down and stay here with me, just in case there is any bother."

What sort of bother? What a crazy, unbalanced lot. Julie thought exasperated…. but she was desperate and would do anything to get home safely. As she looked at the three of them and just nodded. What on earth possessed them to think she could possibly look like Jack, even after the hair styling? The two men returned downstairs, and Aunty started fussing around. "I'll do your hair now, so I'll be ready to open the shop at 9 am."

She produced some alarmingly long-bladed scissors and pulled out a pink velvet stool, which had seen better days. "You can get yourself organised afterwards."

Julie wondered how she could have got this low, and allowed this to happen? She sat on the stool and watched as her beautiful blonde hair was hacked and shaped to look like Jack's. Then the ammonia-smelling dark brown dye was applied.

Aunty thought it was wonderful that she was being such a great help. The whole time she never stopped talking, and with Julie's prompts, she found out a lot more from her which she could tell Clive when she got home, but also things she could investigate for herself. The freedom of getting home and feeling contact with civilisation again.

As Aunty applied the dark thick dollop, she told Julie that she had never been able to have children, and when her sister Audrey had Paul, she had fallen in love with the child almost immediately. Audrey had died when Paul was just three years old and his father, who was in the navy, had a woman on distant shores. When he had been told the sad news about his wife he never returned. So, she had taken Paul on and adopted him as her own. With the village shop being handed down to her through generations she could easily afford to send Paul away for private schooling and give him the good start that she felt he deserved.

"There, all done." She said as she removed the plastic gloves which came free in the box. "Half an hour and you can wash it off."

Leaving the room, she was still locking the door behind her and keeping Julie a prisoner. That 'creak' as she shut the door was really beginning to grate on her. She was so glad tomorrow she wouldn't be hearing it again. She'd be out of here, and back in the real world.

Suddenly a terrible thought struck her. What if she was playing into some sort of game they had planned, and she wasn't going home at all? Paul had told the villagers she had gone home, and Jack was going on vacation with him to Wales. But now she had to pretend to be Jack. What would Mandy have done? Julie asked herself but couldn't find an answer. Paul was extremely persuasive and likeable, people seemed to believe everything he said and hang on his every word. Could he have disposed of Mandy and the other girl, their cousin, Susan?

Although Mandy had dated Paul for a while, and what he had said about nobody knowing anything about him, was true. Julie had learned more about him in the last hour than she had over the year that her sister had been with him. She so wanted to trust him, but she couldn't. Despite his promise to take care of her, and to drive her home, too much had gone on for Julie to truly put her life in his hands.

The alarm went off bringing Julie's thoughts back into the room again, the reminder to wash off the dye from her hair.

Julie was nervous to look in the mirror, but she had to manage to face this…, literally. She was counting the hours until she left this place, this room, this prison. Paul said they would be leaving at 5 am, once The Watchers had gone, and just before The Listeners came out.

Paul had told Julie that The Watchers were creatures who came out in the hours of darkness. They lived in and amongst the marshland and moved about in the shadows and blackness of the night. They were faceless, almost grim reaper-like, with their shapeless bodies and no expression. The Watchers would absorb information and release it among the trees and marshes to The Listeners. Paul had said he thought it was an old wife's tale, until one night when he looked out of the window and saw one.

Julie was very sceptical of the paranormal and wasn't a believer in magic or superstitions. As she dried her hair she was taken aback when she saw the 'new' her in the mirror.

Bringing the long fringe forward and sweeping it across her face there was an uncanny resemblance to Jack. Julie stepped away from the mirror in shock and horror. How did Paul see it, or even come up with this idea? Perhaps being in situations like this before, it was something he was used to. Glancing over at the bed, someone had placed a cap very similar to Jack's for her to wear.

Julie placed a couple of the local history books that she picked up from Aunty's library and placed them into her bag. She would read through them when she returned home.
The footsteps, the creak, the key turning.

"Wow," said Paul entering, "from a distance, you could pass as Jack."

"I thought that was the plan?" Julie replied, dryly.

"Would you like fish and chips?" She nodded. He was gone. Again, that turn of the key. The creak. The footsteps.

Aunty bought up fish and chips with an unopened can of cola.
At least she wasn't going to be drugged this evening. Aunty tried not to look or stare at Julie, who thought she was ashamed of what she had done.

"I'll miss you." She said as she left the room, locking the door behind her. As Julie sat on the bed, tentatively eating her fish and chips, a wave of relief flooded over her. She just needed to get through this night, and then home.

As Julie laid in bed her thoughts started to return, she had heard all three people come up to bed and it had disturbed her sleep. The what ifs and the doubts and the maybes were spinning around in turmoil in her exhausted mind. She had run out of fingernails to chew and began biting at the skin. Gnawing at her thumb quick making it sore until it bled. Coming to reality she realised it was now night and although she was in darkness and needing some toilet paper to wrap around the blood coming from her thumb.

Julie got up from the bed and stumbled towards the bathroom, still half asleep when she saw out of the corner of her eye from the moonlit marshlands a black object moving. She stopped to look at the shapeless black figure moving carefully through the marsh. Then it stopped and turned to face her. There was no face on the wretched creature, just a black blank canvas, no eyes, mouth, or nose. There were no hands, just long batwing arms, and a shapeless body which appeared to glide.

Julie screamed out loud. She didn't realise she could shriek as loudly as she had. Then she fell back smacking her head against the dressing table. Footsteps. Creak. Key turning. Paul and Aunt burst into the room.

"What's happened?" asked Paul. "Did you see a Watcher?" Julie looked straight at him. "I don't know exactly what I saw. From that tale you told me earlier, I guess it must have been. But why are they here looking for me? And how did it know where I was?"

He seemed to have no answer to her questions. Still, she couldn't believe it, and was shocked, and absolutely terrified!

"I don't want to stay here! I don't want to be alone." She was shaking. Whatever Julie had seen had chilled her to the bone.

Aunty had gone to see Jack. Julie heard her say to him that she'd seen one of The Watchers.

"That's why I wanted to give her valarian again this evening." She whispered in a loud voice. "I never wanted her to see them or for them to see her. Now, we're all in trouble." She sounded fearful; she was clearly afraid of something.

Julie heard Jack's terse but kindly reply.

"Remember Aunty you have nothing to worry about anymore, Julie is now me and The Watchers don't know any difference."

But surely, they did, that thing, the shadow with no eyes had stared straight at her! It 'saw' her. It knew her. How can you feel a stare from something that has no eyes?

"Come and sleep in with me." said Paul kindly. "I'll pull out the day bed from underneath mine. You can sleep in my room. I can keep a good eye on you. Does the back of your head hurt where you fell? Are you feeling ok?" He looked genuinely concerned.

Julie nodded, crying. "I just want to go home."

"I know," he said, sounding like he meant it.

Even in Julie's current state, she really wanted him to mean it. He quietly led her into his room, which looked tiny compared to where she had been 'living'. She noticed her bag in the corner of his bedroom, at least that much was true. Paul pulled out a sprung mattress on a wheeled frame from under his bed.

"Hopefully, you'll feel safer here." He dropped on the bed, and in a few moments, Julie could hear his slow, steady breathing.

She lay on the lumpy mattress, for all of his concerns for her now, he hadn't thought to offer her the bed. There were angry wasps filling her head, asking questions. Julie still had so many questions, and not nearly enough answers. But he was right. She felt comfortable, safer in this room with Paul and was so glad they would be leaving by dawn, she didn't care where, she just wanted to be away from the village of Duro. And thinking she would never be able to sleep, she slept. And the wasps finally fell silent.

SEVEN

Paul shook Julie gently awake at dawn and invited her downstairs for breakfast. She couldn't wait to get out. Aunty had given her some hand ointment for her hands and nails, it was a lotion made from beeswax and lavender, from Ma's obviously. It was so soothing on her skin.

Paul took Julie's holdall downstairs. carrying her day bag, she made sure the two local area history books from Aunty's library were safely in there.

Getting into Paul's BMW with its tinted windows was a relief. Julie never even looked back to say goodbye to Aunty. Although she was relieved to finally be leaving this place, she was scared because she had no idea if she was actually being driven to Wales or really being taken home. she prayed it was the latter, and that by the end of the day she'd be back in London, and safe.

Paul was silent. Julie could tell he was very deep in thought. She drifted off and awoke to find them parked up.

"Hey," he said. "Sorry, for everything you went through back there, in Duro. When it all comes to a head, I hope you will realise we only had your safety at heart. Please, can you wear this?" He produced a long blonde wig from the back of the car.

"You were only Jack, to get you out of the village. You can be you again now." She put the wig on and looked straight into the windscreen mirror. Thank goodness she could at least wear this wig until her hair grew back long and to its natural colour again. Despite what she'd been through, and what she'd seen, there was also the constant nagging thought at the back of her mind she still hadn't found Mandy, or Ma.

Paul brought her bag from the car and followed her to her flat. It was so nice to be back home. She just wanted a nice cup of tea, a bath, and to sleep. Then, tomorrow a fresh start.

"I'm just going to get some food." Said Paul. Julie turned her head sharply.

"What?" She answered with surprise. "When did *we* come into the equation?" He threw his head back and laughed. "You didn't think I would just be dropping you off, then driving back, did you? Did you seriously think I'd be leaving you alone? Now of all times."

Julie didn't know what to think, and whether this was what she really wanted. She had been through a lot of traumas which would take her a long while to get over her ordeals. And despite all his kind words and reassurances, she still didn't and couldn't feel she could fully trust him. She truly wanted to, she needed to believe she had a friend watching out for her.

Julie knew he was doing something, but what?

Julie was exhausted and drifted off, waking up to the wonderful smell of Chinese food wafting from the kitchen. She picked herself up from the sofa.

"I didn't know you could cook Chinese food?" She smiled as Paul appeared from the kitchen carrying a tray of dishes.

"No." He laughed. "I picked one up from your local takeaway. I'm going to stay here for a few days. I'll stay in Mandy's room. I'll work from here; I also want to see if I've missed anything about her disappearance. Duro village thinks I've gone to Wales with Jack, remember?" Paul looked over at her. "I don't think Mandy is alive." He said with tears in his eyes.

"Do you think she drowned?" Julie queried.

He nodded but added, "I just think it's odd that Susan and Mandy both came looking for their same ancestors and ended up presumably drowning. I can't believe it. But I have been through the situation over and over again. I've gone all over the area and have come up with nothing.

"I spoke to Clive the detective on the case from here and again he has come up with nothing either."

They ate their food in silence, both wrapped up their thoughts.

"To think I'll never see Mandy again is something I just can't get my head around." Julie said, sadly.

Paul hung his head and just nodded.

"I'd like Clive to come around and for all three of us to go through everything again. I want to tell him and you everything that I saw and what Mandy had told me through her phone calls. Just one more time. Maybe, just maybe someone can shed some light on the situation, something we may have missed. Please," Julie begged him. "Just one more time."

Julie decided to keep her loungers on a red tartan trouser with a red skinny rib top in brushed cotton. She was anxious but excited to eventually after all this time, to be able to switch her phone and laptop on at last, and actually have an internet signal.

Paul hadn't told her how long she'd been kept at Aunty's. Julie felt it must have been a long as her inbox was completely overloaded.

Julie was hoping to have received some message from Mandy or Clive, but there was nothing, only work messages and a couple from Angela just asking when she would be back to meet up.

She had contacted work, and without going into too much detail had let them know what had been going on. Her boss had given her the opportunity to work from home, which suited Julie down to the ground, allowing time to try and find herself again.

Julie phoned Clive to arrange a meeting between her and Paul, wanting to tell him about the area and the villagers, and about Paul's aunt. Paul had already beaten her to it and had arranged for them to meet at hers. Clive wouldn't be free for a few weeks. He didn't seem interested, and as she hadn't come across anything which he thought was enough to re-open the case, he still considered the case closed.

She didn't tell Paul all of the information that his aunt had told her, as some of her tales seemed so untrue. Nevertheless, Julie decided to put it into a search engine for Golden Blood or the Blood of the Gods. She was extremely shocked by what she found.

'In Ancient Greece, it was thought the gods had golden blood. Called Ichor, this ethereal fluid was fabled to have immortal properties but was toxic to mere mortals.

Until a person with "golden blood" was discovered.

This blood is so special as it is excellent for transfusion because it lacks common antigens, and it can be accepted by anyone who needs a transfusion without the risk of a blood transfusion reaction. However, due to its rarity, it gets extremely difficult to find this type.

Blood is considered RH-null if it lacks all of the 61 possible antigens in the RH system. It is also very dangerous to live with this blood type, as so few people have it.

Because Rh-null lacks all 61 possible antigens, it can be donated to people who have blood types that are very different from the main eight. However, Rh-null can only accept blood from people with the Rh-null blood type.

The scarcity of Rh-null blood, combined with its unique properties, makes it extremely valuable for scientific research, earning its name "Golden Blood."

Unlike other blood types, people with Rh Null blood have no Rh antigens on their red blood cells.

Healthcare professionals classify blood type according to the presence or absence of antigens, which are proteins attached to red blood cells.

RHAG mutation is often associated with a disease called hereditary stomatocytosis. These individuals can have long-term, mild, haemolytic anaemia and increased RBC breakdown. The Rh-null phenotype can also be seen in the case of certain anaemias a person may be born with.

The following conditions may put you at a higher risk of the golden blood group:

Consanguineous marriage (marriage between cousins, brother-sister, or anybody who is a near or distant relative).

Was this the blood disorder her dad had? She wondered. Aunty had said her grandmother and grandfather had been cousins as had their own parents. Maybe he had been born with this blood type and had passed it down. Perhaps Susan's mother had it? And what if Pauls' mother had it also?

There were too many maybes and perhaps, but it did make a lot of sense.

It still didn't throw any light on Mandy's or Susan's disappearances. She also wondered if Paul's aunt had known in depth about the rare blood condition, or whether it was just local gossip, and she knew nothing else about it.

Printing off the documents she filed them along with all the other information she had collected and written down while in Duro. Just the name Duro chilled her to the bone. Taking the ghastly, cheap wig off, it was making her scalp itch. She dared herself to look in the mirror. She still couldn't get over how she had allowed her beautiful blonde hair to be hacked and dyed dark brown. She looked nothing like Jack, why on earth had she believed in them?

She scouted through her emails again…. Nothing brought her closer to finding her sister. She looked at all her missed calls, they were all numbers she recognised. She went through all the text messages and voicemails, but all were recognisable. and nothing at all to put her onto her sister's disappearance.

She flopped onto the bed, she just couldn't let this go, there was nothing of Mandy's or Susan's, nothing had been washed up onto the riverbank.

Julie picked up one of the books she had borrowed from Paul's aunt, the one that was old and focussed on the local Duro history. She hadn't opened it yet, but the cover and title interested her. She thought it may have something about the golden blood, Ma's land, and the monks of Duro Rock. She was also hoping it may have something on the tales of The Watchers and The Listeners.

She was still trying to fathom what she had seen in the marshes at Aunty's house. She was having day and nightmares about what she had seen that dark, windswept night. Just remembering the faceless figure, turn and look at her. She shivered, and her pulse raced.

EIGHT

The dark blue leather-bound book had no author or publisher. On its cover just DURO in gold-gilded writing. The first double page showed an old map of the River Duro with its East and West boundaries. Julie noticed Ma's land had once been called The Pastures, The Gateway had been a tavern. A separate map showed Duro Rock. Each place had its own chapter. It was a book within a book, and she couldn't wait to read it.

Paul had laughed at her when she had shown him. "Does it also show an X marks the spot?" He had said with sarcasm.

Julie just ignored him and started to read. Some of the writings were written in Gaelic and for this she would have to find a way to translate.

Duro

Duro was a dreamy hamlet hidden and lost in the suburbs with roughly a few hundred villagers all working together to support the local community.
The River Duro meandered through the hamlet dividing Duro into three parts. The Rock, The Pastures, and The Gateway Inn, which was nestled on the riverbank next to the jetty and two miles from Duro Village.

In the village was a church and a school. The local shop was also the post office. Next door to this was a chemist for the locals.

The Pastures were on the far side of the River Duro and grew most of the local produce which was sold in The Great Barn next to The Gateway Inn.

The area was surrounded by marsh and wetlands. The River Duro meandered through the hamlet flowing out into an outlet towards Duro Rock.

The Pastures.

As far back as records show The Pastures were owned by farmers of The Sonning Family, who cultivated herbs and spices. Marketing their produce with the Duro Monks, along with their natural pharmaceutical products that were distributed offshore and sold among the villagers.

There was suspicion of witchcraft and Wicca's doings in The Pastures. Some folks have said that The Watchers and The Listeners were brought to life one night when their magic went too far and out of control, bringing life to monstrous black shapes that only appeared in the darkness of shadows and became lost souls hiding, only existing beyond, and living in the marshes.

No-one had ever seen a Listener. It was said they were invisible to the human eye, but if any villagers needed a message sent, it was said to be carried through the trees and on the breeze by The Listeners.

Julie needed a breather. It was a very strange book and a lot to take in. She made herself a coffee and Paul joined her. She cleared her throat.

"Paul?" she asked. "Has Aunty ever talked to you about my grandparents? Have you ever asked her? She said she went to school with them, and they fell in love at an early age, got married and she never saw my granddad again. She said he had the golden blood."

Paul looked down into his empty cup. Silent, like he was holding something back.

He shook his head. "Nope," he said, "never heard of it. Although in my research I did find out they were married young and your fathers' parents, your grandparents were cousins, and your grandfather had a brother, but no one knew what happened to him. He was a lot younger. Apparently, their grandparents were second cousins. Villagers said it was so they could keep their land and The Gateway in the family."

"So, how did my granddad die?" She asked.

"I've no idea," he replied, quietly. "I was always under the impression his parents sold The Gateway, and they all moved to live at The Pastures with Ma and her family, but" he added. "That, I'm not really certain of." He glanced at her, almost sheepishly.

"Please believe me, Julie, if I knew anything more, I'd tell you. I promise you that." He gently took her hand. And for the first time, she felt she saw a glimpse of honesty in his eyes.

She stood up and walked into the kitchen. Feeling mentally and physically stronger than she had for some time. More than that, she was ravenous.

"Full English?" she asked, "please tell me we're having a fry up." Paul looked over at her and smiled.

"Your wish is my command, be ready in a few minutes. Coffee's already good to go."

Although Paul was her best hope, Julie still wasn't ready to share her research with him. She'd wait until Clive was with them and they could all lay their cards on the table.

Over breakfast Julie asked, "Do you think The Watchers are lost souls raised from devil worship and witchcraft?"

"What a load of nonsense," he answered. "What kind of rubbish are you reading?"

"Well, we have both seen them," she replied, indignantly. "What do *you* think they are?" He shrugged his shoulders.

"Maybe it was just a shadow, and we want to believe and imagine we see them."

Julie ignored him. She knew what she saw! She nodded looking over at him as she drank her coffee. He sighed and got up, heading back to Mandy's bedroom.

"Thanks," he said as he walked away, without looking back, "I needed that coffee."

Sitting back on the grey velvet sofa, arranging the yellow and grey cushions behind her back for comfort and with outstretched legs resting on the yellow Chesterfield footstool, she reached out for the book again. The next chapter immediately drew her in further.

The Gateway.

Run by The Saltern family. Through generations of cousins and marriage, it was used by travellers who would pick up mead, spices, and pharmaceutical compounds, some of which contained illegal properties. Nobody really knew how much money they made, or what substances were available. By all accounts it was a very secretive affair.

The local Monks stored their locally made mead, along with their home brewed whiskeys; distilled from local potatoes and wheat, in the basement of the tavern.

Julie stopped short. Basement? She thought, under The

Gateway Pub? How come Paul, Clive, and his team hadn't checked the basement for clues? She added this to her notepad, something else she would bring up at the meeting.

The River Duro

The river entered the village which meandered towards The Rock emptying into the sea from its mouth. Travellers, locals, and traders would use this wonderful river The Duro, which is the Gaelic word for Gateway. The name was used as its nickname, and stuck.

What!? She re-read Duro as the area and the river's nickname. So it was all called The Gateway, and so it was all connected? It *must* be in some way. Julie was so glad she'd picked up this book to read. There were so many questions she needed to ask., she wondered if Aunty knew any of this – she must know. Surely? If the monks used to hide their wares in the cellar what could be hidden in there now?

She grudgingly put the book to one side., went to the kitchen and poured herself a large, chilled Pinot and opened a bag of peanuts.

How come it was only her, just an ordinary person with no forensic or detective training, who had stumbled across information. If she had the authority and back-up, she would follow the leads she came across, but it seemed that no one was interested in the case anymore.

The next part of the book followed the river's journey written about the houseboats moored up on its banks of The Gateway Tavern side, making way for traders using the jetty.

Duro Rock

Also once known as Gateway Rock, or The Innis where monks lived and worked.

To reach the island one would have to sail around to the far side which brings you to a wide-open river delta before going into the sea. The large mooring area and the beauty of the rock formation of the abbey brought travellers from far and wide.

For traders, sailing from the open ocean, The Rock was the first thing they saw, sheltering the Duro hamlet. To the left would bring them to the jetty and Gateway Tavern. To the right side of Duro Rock were The Pastures, which were private property. By invite only. Small boats could be moored, usually by the monks to pick, harvest and cultivate drugs, herbs, and spices.

Traders boats would moor at The Rock to trade their wares of gold, and silver, and to receive cures and herbal drugs and some opioids, so addictions leading to dependency were commonplace, and inevitable. Duro became a very rich hamlet.

She was hoping the book would have mentioned how many children The Saltern family had or about the Golden Blood. But for some reason there was no mention.

She couldn't help wondering when her Mum started to research looking for her dad's family or whether she or dad's adopted family had known anything about The Salterns and had decided not to share the information with anyone, knowing if they had, it would have and had opened a can of worms. Like it is now!

Placing the book into her folder, she hoped Clive would re-open the case.

NINE

Weeks had gone by, and Clive said he would be arranging the meeting for the middle of next week. Paul said he would stay until then. He had been busy with other work and had been supporting her too. He never mentioned Duro, her sister, or what had happened there.

It had affected Julie's mental health. Apart from the front door she always left doors open, even in the bathroom. Maybe one day she would understand why his aunt had locked her in that room.

Although she was looked after to a certain degree, she had also been drugged every night and locked in like a prisoner, never knowing when someone would come to see her, or what would happen next. Only knowing that her life was in danger. Seeing one of The Watchers had seriously unnerved her and had put her close to the edge. Julie knew what she'd seen! That wretched faceless shape, although Paul tried to convince her otherwise, saying The Watchers and The Listeners were a local urban myth, to scare people away from The Hamlet.

Julie went back to work part-time but couldn't focus on anything but her sister. Constantly looking at her mobile in case Mandy had tried to get in touch. The company was great, clearly recognising that she was having real trouble dealing with something, although they didn't know the full details. They suggested a leave of absence for a few months.

Even Angela, Julie's neighbour, and friend was getting tired of her constant thoughts and theories about what had happened to Mandy.

"Come on, Jules," she said one evening. "I know it's easy for me to say, but you just need to try and move on. I get how difficult that must be, but it's tearing you up. I can see it ripping you apart from the inside. You're my friend, and I don't know what I can do to help." There were genuine tears in her eyes.

Julie nodded, not replying. She ate, slept, and dreamt about her sister. Sometimes she would have night terrors, dreaming of running through dark long corridors searching for her, as she heard her screaming her name. But could never find her. Julie woke up, exhausted and sweating.

The day was fast approaching when Clive and Paul would be meeting here to listen to her story, and for why she thought the case should be reopened. Her hair had started to grow out, she had applied bleach on top of the brown which had turned her hair an orange colour. Julie thought she looked odd. So booked herself into a salon, for a full treatment. She sat in the stylist's chair, saying simply.

"Do what you want with it, I need a new start, and what better way than a makeover." The hairdresser smiled, and Julie smiled back.

The stylist certainly did that, with a short urchin cut finishing off with a toner, giving the overall finish a natural colour with a short blonde spiky texture of woven highlights.

Julie finished off with a deep facial. Returning home, she felt like a million dollars.

Feeling mentally stronger than she had for a long time, she vacuumed through, dusted around. She re-read her notes and arranged them in date order.

Julie hadn't seen Paul for a week, so he was shocked when he turned up.

"Wow, Jules." He exclaimed. "You look sensational, I didn't recognise you." She secretly smiled, it was just the lift she needed. She didn't like being called Jules. Only her friends were allowed to call her that. And she still didn't think of Paul as a friend.

At last, Clive arrived, the coffee had percolated, the timing was perfect. She put a tray on the square coffee table. White China mugs at the ready, a jug of cream, and made sure she had provided sugar cubes. Paul always finished his meals with coffee like this and always made a point of saying.

"Coffee with cream and two sugar cubes." He was so fussy and had been spoilt by his Aunty's upbringing.

Julie placed the biscotti biscuits on a large plate, having put every effort into this, hoping the men would agree with what she was about to say. She was nervous, slowly sitting down, and placing her notes on her lap.

Clive kept looking over at her as he reached forward to pour a coffee.

"You look very different," he said, questioningly. "The new look suits you."

Before Julie had time to reply.

"So, what's the urgency?" he said. "I'm an extremely busy man."

He looked very official as he took a Dictaphone from his pocket and placed it on the table between them. Slowly recording today's date, time, and who was sitting in the room.

Wow, Julie thought, she'd expected an informal meeting, not an interrogation. She suddenly felt extremely shy and nervous, and as she started to speak, her anxiety levels rose even further. She felt stupid.

She began to speak about when she had first arrived at The Gateway, using the pub phone as there was no internet connection.

"Yes," Clive interrupted, "My team and I found that out when we were investigating your sister's disappearance."

She told Clive that she'd met a guy called Jack who owned and moored his boat Jackie, alongside the River Duro, taking passengers to and from The Gateway jetty to Duro Rock. She told him about visiting The Rock and how she thought she had seen Paul through the viewfinder on the island. She told how she had been drugged at The Gateway. Bizarrely remembering the cleanliness of the telephone sitting on the bar. How she had stayed with Paul's Aunty, being locked in a room unknowingly being dosed with valerian every night.

"Apparently, my life was in danger," said Julie. Paul shifted uncomfortably in his seat, as Clive sharply interrupted.

"And why was that?" Clive looked over at Paul for answers.

"It was for her protection, that's all, what with Susan and then Mandy, my aunt and I were concerned. And Julie," added Paul looking at Clive. "I think you thought you were locked up as a prisoner." Clive looked at Paul.

"She truly wasn't locked up," said Paul to Clive. "My Aunt looked after Julie, she was clearly neurotic, so Aunty gave a light sedative to calm and rest her. She was making up, seeing shapes and shadows and freaking out. It was unsettling."

Julie told Clive that Paul and Aunty had cut and dyed her hair, so she looked like Jack. She went on to talk about The Watchers and The Listeners, saying that she had seen one. Despite Paul's doubting words, Julie knew what she had seen.

She showed the beautifully blue leather-bound book about Duro and read out its contents. She also mentioned the Golden Blood, supposedly being the blood of the gods.

When she had finished reminiscing, Clive asked her if she had found any new evidence about what could have happened to her sister. In fact, had she actually found anything, which would warrant reopening the investigation? Julie shook her head. She felt dazed and like she had been slapped.

Paul raised his eyebrows and shook his head when she mentioned The Watchers and The Listeners, and then carried on talking about the blood of the gods.

Clive switched off his recorder after recording the time of the finished interview.

"It seems to me, Julie." He said bluntly, but calmly. "You seem to have lost your way, I can see your mental health has clearly suffered from the loss of your sister, and I can understand that, but I think you need to seek professional help. You have also wasted police time. You have not shown any new evidence. Nothing you have said today, gives me reason to re-open your sister's case. I'm sorry to sound harsh, but you need help and to come to terms that your sister unfortunately isn't coming home. I know it's tragic, but I just can't re-open the case with what you have told me. However, if you want to open a new investigation into Paul and Aunty's treatment of you, that's up to you. It would have to be treated as a totally separate case."

Julie was devastated and started to cry. Paul handed her the bag at the side of the sofa; it was the one she had taken with her to Duro and had forgotten it was there.

"Here," he said, with gritted teeth, "looks like there is a large serviette sticking out the top, use it to dry your eyes."

Opening the large serviette, she remembered putting the thread from Mandy's coat which she'd found behind the bar, and safely placed it into a napkin. Opening up the fold where she'd so carefully laid it. Julie showed Paul and Clive.

"See?" She cried out triumphantly. "Evidence!"

"How?" asked Clive. "How is this evidence? You've removed this cotton strand from where it was, and you are trying to convince me that it came from Mandy's coat and is evidence that she stayed at The Gateway, which." He added. "We already know." He got up to leave. "Seriously, Julie. You need to see a doctor. Please don't waste mine or any more police time." Clive put the recorder into his briefcase and left.

Julie was absolutely devastated. Paul sat there just looking at her. Julie could sense that he was angry.

"Well?" She asked.

"Well, what?" He replied. "I thought you were going to give evidence on something to show you have found where or what happened to Mandy. Instead, all you did was talk nonsense. And as for you? What exactly are *you* playing at?"

Julie just sat with her head buried in the large soft napkin, crying.

Paul picked up the tartan thread which she had placed on the table.

"Where did you say you found this?" He asked. "And Clive was right, if it had been a piece of evidence, you should have left it, and just taken a photo of the proof."

"I found it on the other side of the bar at The Gateway." She sniffed as she blew her nose. "I saw it on the far side of the bar just above the cellar latch. I wondered why it would be there, and not the bar side." Paul twirled it between his fingers.

"It's definitely Mandy's, who on earth could forget that awful orange and green tartan jacket. Could it mean anything?" She almost hesitated to ask. Unsure of his reaction.

Paul replied. "Seriously Julie, it's painful enough that this happened. I think the same as Clive, I think you need some help and mental support. If this piece of thread is evidence, you have tampered with it and by removing it, could have removed a vital piece of information." He said grimly.

"What shall I do?" Julie almost whimpered.

"Go see a shrink." He answered and left without a glance or another word.

TEN

Sitting in the doctor's surgery waiting for her appointment, looking around at the patients in the room, observing them, and wondering if anyone here had experienced a family disappearance, and if so, how they had dealt with it.

Everyone sitting here was lost in their own thoughts and dreams. Plenty of coughs, she secretly smiled to herself. Funny that, if there was a room with people surrounded by quietness one would always hear a cough here and there. From nowhere, it brought up a happy memory of her dad who always mentioned it when they used to sit watching the snooker together, there was always someone who coughed in the silence.

On the waiting room walls were adverts for CRISIS, well-being, counselling phone numbers, or other contact details with email addresses attached.

Perhaps she should contact some of these, although they might think she was so broken and needed locking up. Just the idea was terrifying. Julie's thoughts were becoming morbid, trying to think of something other than the loss of Mandy. But every thought led back to her. What was she to do? She'd contacted Paul, but he wasn't returning her calls or texts. Even leaving him a message telling him she'd taken his advice and was seeing her GP today. Another cough. She smiled.

Even though Julie was trying to move on, the night terrors were starting to enter her daily thoughts. She would shake and sweat. The dream would always be the same, always running through dark dimly lit corridors with Mandy crying and calling out "Help me!" Julie would try and follow her sister's frantic calls. But every turn she took seemed to take her further away from Mandy's frantic calls, until it was a distant whimper. She was also having increasingly unpleasant thoughts about The Watcher she had seen. The faceless creature was constantly playing on her mind.

Julie's GP was very understanding and sympathetic. She prescribed her medication and sent a referral email to the local Psychiatric Unit, headed 'For Urgent Attention'.

She should receive a phone call in the next few weeks. In the meantime, the GP handed her some leaflets with useful phone numbers, in case she needed more support before the appointment came through.

Over the following few weeks, she phoned the support therapy team who were extremely helpful, they didn't cure you but supported you and were always understanding. She screamed, cried and laughed with helpless frustration, reliving the anxiety and traumas she had suffered in Duro.

Julie was slowly learning how to get normality and control back into her life again – albeit without Mandy.

She visited her local church, something she had never done before and spoke to the pastor. Although there was no body to bury, he suggested a service to celebrate Mandy's life, which lifted her spirits, making her feel stronger in mind and soul.

Having no family, Julie just invited her and Mandy's friends and colleagues. She left a message on Paul's mobile inviting him to the celebration of Mandy's life, but there was no reply.

The day was bright, and the sun shone. A small congregation arrived at the church all with Mandy's favourite colour flowers, purple.

The colour and the fragrance of the lavender, verbena, salvias, sweet peas, pansies, and statice filled the small church. Julie put a large photograph of Mandy up, her warm smile filled with love, warmth, and fun. At the side of the photograph, she placed a vase of Lilac Roses; Blue Moon and Blue for You. Mandy had always loved roses.

The congregation sang Morning has Broken by Cat Stevens, the pastor read a piece about Mandy finishing with a prayer of hope. If she was still alive and had wanted to make a new life somewhere, that all was ok with God, and she would always be forgiven, her friends prayed and wished her well in her new life wherever that might be.

After the service, the congregation supported her by visiting a park Mandy liked to walk through. They planted a buddleia in remembrance of her life and placed the bouquets and beautiful sprigs next to the purple butterfly tree at the place of rest.

They wanted to finish the day on a happier note so they all went to Mandy's favourite hangout, and just laughed about the happier times and all the things she would get up to. They all wrote their memories into a book that had been left on the bar.

A lot of friends agreed with her that they didn't think Mandy had died but they had to say their goodbyes to her and move on. Angela had thought all this might help Julie reminisce and eventually heal, and to just remember the good times.

Angela checked up on her most evenings to make sure she was ok; they would usually end up having supper together. Julie wasn't sure what she would have done without her dear friend.

She was in two minds as to whether to take the medication her GP had prescribed. The first time she had taken one of the pills, she felt like she'd lost touch with reality. And with Angela here living opposite, she finally started to feel that she was doing ok.

Julie still hadn't heard from Paul, although she had tried to keep in contact with him. He hadn't returned any calls, messages and hadn't even sent a card or flowers to the celebration of Mandy's life. She was upset by this and had decided she would not contact him again. There was clearly no point, he wasn't replying to her, and obviously just wanted to forget and move on.

Time had passed. Julie had finally come to terms with the fact that Mandy was never coming home. She was in the kitchen boiling the kettle and waiting for Angela. They both had the morning off, and Angela had gone to buy some croissants from the new bakery when she heard the landline ring. It made her jump. No-one called on the main number! It hadn't rung for years, and she'd forgotten they still had it.

It had been the same number they had growing up and when their parents had passed away Mandy and her decided to keep the phone number. The number was so easy to remember, and as children they would race to see who could say the number the quickest.

The telephone was kept in Mandy's bedroom, she would use it as her work phone, so Julie had no reason to use it. Even though Mandy had gone. Her bedroom was exactly the same as it had been left on the morning she'd stormed out and left for Duro. Although they'd been close, she still felt like an intruder when entering the room.

Grabbing the phone, Julie thought, could it be Mandy? No, she had to put that thought out of her mind.

"Hello?" She almost shouted.

"Oh hello," said a rather posh voice. "Is this Julie Salturns?"

"Yes?" she replied with a question mark.

"This is Dr Smythe's secretary, sorry it's taken a while to contact you. There was quite a long waiting list, but I've been informed you've had support and help from therapists on the telephone. Am I correct in saying your GP has prescribed you some medication to help with your sleeping?"

"Yes?" she replied again, with another question mark. She was completely nonplussed by the call, although she'd been expecting it.

After asking her to verify full name, date of birth, and address she asked Julie if she could give her a little more detail about the grief she was feeling over the loss of her sister.

"We will phone again on this number next week to make an appointment." The phone clicked.

Julie wondered why the psychiatrist's secretary had phoned the home phone number, but then she remembered neither Mandy nor her had updated their medical records to their mobile numbers, but the landline still worked just as well.

She had a sudden thought though, what if Mandy had left a message on this line or had tried calling when she'd been in Duro? Mandy didn't know Julie had come looking for her and may have tried to contact her. She dialled to listen to any messages. There weren't any.

Of course, why would there be? Mandy was gone. She was delusional to think she was still coming home.

Feeling completely lost she anxiously waited for Angela to get back. Angela knew Julie well enough to know when something wasn't right. Over breakfast she invited herself over to supper that night. Julie agreed immediately, it would keep her busy and brain occupied while awaiting her company.

The thought of Paul still niggled. No contact at all after that meeting. Maybe that's for the best anyway she thought, on reflection.

Cooking relaxed her with the radio on loud.

The evening couldn't come too soon. With a tap on the door, Angela walked in with a bottle of their favourite wine, a nice fruity red. A perfect accompaniment to the spaghetti Bolognese she had made. All was good.

"I need to ask you something?" Angela asked hesitantly. "You can say no, but please can I read that book about Duro?"

"Um, of course," she replied, slightly quizzical. Glancing over her shoulder at Angela.

"Oh, I hoped you wouldn't mind." She answered, as the wine was being poured. "It's just I've shared the journey with you and would love to read about the area, especially now that things have died down." Julie nodded and reached over to the bookcase to pick up the book.

"There," she smiled as she handed Angela the book. "Keep it for as long as you like."

As Angela opened the book and started to flip through, one of the pages wouldn't bend the same as the others. "The paper on this page is different, thicker, and doesn't blend like the others," said Angela. "Look!"

Intrigued, Julie walked over and peered at the book. Angela flicked the pages again. Sure enough, the paper near the back seemed thicker than the others as if it was made from a material other than paper, it was almost like a card.

"What is it?" She asked Angela. "Why is it like that?"

Angela shrugged her shoulders. "I'm not sure, Jules. It's almost as if two pages have been glued together like an envelope with something in the middle." Julie just turned to stare at her.

She went to the kitchen drawer and took out her scissors.

"Here," she said, handing them to Angela. "Let's cut out the page."

Angela stared back at her, "sure?" She asked. There was real tension in the room. Julie smiled back and nodded.

Carefully and with a trembling hand, Angela cut the page as close to the book spine as possible. The page unravelled to expose a hidden pocket.

Holding her breath, Julie watched Angela slowly and gingerly take out the contents. Her heart missed a beat, and her pulse started to race.

"You've gone white." said Angela, looking over, but holding something in her fingers. "I'll get you some water."

Sipping the water, Julie wasn't sure if she could or was ready to deal with any more surprises or shocks. Once the colour had returned to her cheeks and her breathing was back to normal, Angela asked if she wanted her to open it

Julie nodded but still not sure if she wanted to see. She didn't know what to expect.

"You open it, please." Angela understood and carefully opened the contents.

Angela hesitantly pulled out the piece of paper, which was folded neatly to match the exact page size. As she started to unfold the paper, it was clear there was a hand-drawn map.

"Where and what is this place?" Angela looked down, and gasped. "Is this Duro?" She looked at Julie, questioningly.

As Julie looked, she instinctively knew it was Duro. The map appeared to show a tunnel of mazes that went from The Gateway to Ma's Pastures. The tunnels channelled under the River Duro, with other pathways, seemingly always leading to Ma's. Farmhouse.

"This must have been where The Duro monks kept their wares and opioids?" she thought out loud.

"Do you think the tunnels are still there?" Asked Angela.

"I doubt it very much," she replied. "I think it's just an old map that traders would use to sell and hide their illicit dealings."

"What a great piece of history we have stumbled on." Smiled Angela, clearly very excited, lifting her glass for a 'cheers'.

"I wonder how many of these books with hidden maps were put together?" she replied, raising her glass to meet Angela's. They were both grinning.

"I don't know, but…," she added adamantly. "We aren't going to investigate to find out either."

The rest of the evening was spent looking at the map. The spaghetti was almost forgotten.

"Angela?" Julie said. "This map is just between us, ok?' I'm not going to contact Paul or Clive about it. The last time I mentioned anything, I was told I was wasting valuable police time." Angela squeezed her arm reassuringly.

"It's ok," she nodded, kindly, "This goes nowhere."

As Angela got up to leave, she picked up the book and the map.

"I'm taking these home with me," she said, in a voice that didn't invite any further discussion. Julie was happy to let her take them. Weirdly, the flat felt cleaner with them gone.

She tossed and turned, another night terror making her sleep thready and unrestful. Julie woke, feeling unsettled. but couldn't exactly say why. Sitting on the side of the bed, coming to, she wondered if she'd started to overthink again. What if Mandy was trapped in a tunnel and got lost? Her slowly mending mind began to spiral uncontrollably. Should she return to Duro? Perhaps she should visit Aunty, Paul and Jack? Julie just didn't know what the next step was. Should she talk to Angela? She knew she should, she'd been with her all the way through this... Yes, she would tell her.

The following week her thoughts had become clearer, and she had decided what she was going to do. When she told Angela, she just smiled. A warm, loving smile. A look that only a real friend can give.

All she said was. "I'm coming with you."

Julie woke early, another night terror left her breathless and sweating, but she didn't really know what she had been dreaming about to make her feel this disorientated. She sat on the edge of the bed, and slowly gathered herself for the day. She popped a pill. Something she was getting used to.

With the early sun shining through the crack in the satin grey curtains, she got up and made a pot of tea: half Twining's loose-leaf English Breakfast tea and half Earl Grey - or *Lady Grey* as Mandy had jokingly called it when Paul had introduced her and Julie to his morning routine. The delicate jasmine flavour certainly gave a great taste to the start of a new day.

Still in an early morning daze, Julie switched the television on, more for company rather than interest, and idly flicked through the channels. She just wanted a voice. Someone to talk to her, although the words meant nothing.

She ate breakfast and dozed off again, jumping awake with a start when the landline rang again. Glancing over at the clock, it was nearly 8 am. She ran to get the phone; she needed this appointment.

"Hello," she panted. "Sorry I took so long to get to the phone; I didn't realise you were going to phone me back so early in the morning." Expecting to hear the receptionist's voice.

At first, there was silence, then…

"Help me," whispered a pleading, weak voice. "Please, help me!" A voice she knew immediately. A voice she had convinced herself she'd never hear again. She went cold, and then she started to sweat. Julie started shaking.

"Mandy, is this you? Where are you? What's going on? I'm coming…"

There was a click, ending the connection. She had to talk to Angela, as she picked herself up, she fell again. Her mind couldn't process what had just happened. She fainted away, and didn't remember hitting the floor.

ELEVEN

When Julie came to, picking herself up, she took another pill, and went over to Angela's immediately.

Angela's pure white painted apartment had a slightly larger layout than hers and would have looked clinical and austere but the added black framed mirrors and fern green furnishings had made her living space modern but welcoming.

Angela couldn't make sense of what Julie was saying as she opened her door. Julie stood there in a long black nightdress. Shaking, crying, and stuttering.

"Come in! Come in!" Angela said, pulling her in. "You look like you've seen a ghost. It wasn't one of those Listeners or Watchers, was it?"

Angela said she had been up most of the night reading Duro and was fascinated by it. She put the kettle on, made Julie a sweet cup of tea, and placed some of her favourite chocolate biscuits on a plate. Draping a warm bright pink dressing gown around her shoulders and making a quick telephone call to let work know Julie was having the rest of the day off. Thankfully she was due to work from home that day. Angela came and sat beside her. Her warmth made Julie feel better, comfortable and more importantly, she felt safe.

"Look here, young lady," Angela said sternly, "once you have calmed down, you need to tell me or write down what has happened."

It took Julie a full hour to calm herself enough to be able to coherently tell Angela what had happened.

Angela's hazel eyes opened wider than Julie could ever imagine as she told her that she'd heard Mandy's voice asking for help.

"Are you sure it was really Mandy, Jules?" She asked., hesitantly.

Julie answered slowly, "I know I was half asleep, and last night I took another pill, but I'm certain it was Mandy."

"I believe you," said Angela. "Right! Let's go and save your sister." Julie raised her eyebrows not quite believing what she'd heard.

Angela immediately took over. "Look," she said. "I've known you and Mandy for years, and I know you may do some strange things, but honestly you aren't mad or anything else along those lines. I don't believe that for a minute. You're my best friend, besides, it will be an adventure and to be honest, I really need a break from work." She smiled, playfully. Despite the situation, Julie couldn't help smiling back.

Angela suggested that Julie go home, shower and get dressed. In the meantime, she would organise the time off from work. She'd also mentioned a few ideas that she asked Julie to think about before she came round that afternoon.

"And this time, Jules," Angela said firmly, "No police and no Paul… I insist." Julie nodded in agreement. Relieved that someone was finally taking control.

"Thanks for believing in me, Angela." She smiled, before returning to her flat.

After showering and throwing on her old navy-blue velour Juicy Couture tracksuit. The one that she would often come home after work to find Mandy wearing. They had shared most clothes, but this tracksuit was hers. It smelt of Mandy's perfume, Dylan Blue by Givenchy, the sweet floral notes of Forget-me-not hues.

"Oh Mandy," Julie whispered out loud. "How could I forget you? And now I'm coming to find you and I'm going to bring you home to safety."

As Julie sat on the sofa waiting for Angela, she started to doubt what she'd heard. The voice on the telephone sounded like Mandy but was spine-chilling, and almost disconnected, similar to the voice she was hearing in her night and day terrors. Her gut feeling told her instinctively it was Mandy. Julie wasn't sure if she'd imagined her sister's voice, because that was what she wished for so badly. Her thoughts had become jumbled - but that voice…. *Help Me…* chilled Julie to the core.

An expected a tap at the door made her jump.

"Hi Jules," said Angela, walking in excitedly, "I've had a few ideas on how to find that sister of yours and how to get her home. She held the Duro book and map, along with pen and paper.

As she sat next to Julie, Angela noticed she had packed a small bag already to leave.

"We can't go today, Jules," she said, shaking back her shoulder length highlighted hair. "Mandy has been missing for ages, and now we've suddenly found out there might be a chance she is still alive. If we try to look for her with no backup plan, we could go missing, too. Remember we may even find Susan, your cousin who also went missing in the same area. And who knows, your Grandmother Monica could need rescuing too."

Julie knew she was right, and as her friend laid out the map and put her writing pad on the table. Julie was eager to listen and ready to hear her plan of action.

Angela had a slightly unconventional brother, Ned, who lived in a campervan and travelled from place to place picking up odd jobs. He loved being outside. A lot of people called him a drifter, but he didn't seem to care what people thought. Julie had never met him but heard lots of tales about him from Angela on their prosecco evenings.

Angela's idea was to park up at The Gateway alongside the other campervans. Julie had decided to wear her hair even shorter and dye it a deep auburn hoping she would be unrecognisable. No one had met Angela, not even Paul. They would change their names to Anna and Emma and ask at The Gateway if there was any temporary bar work. The plan would be for them to get to the pub cellar surreptitiously, then try and find the door that would take them to the tunnel leading to The Pastures and on to Ma's place, as shown on the map.

Julie would go first and if she didn't come back, Angela and her brother would drive out of Duro until they had a phone signal. Then they would call Clive and let him know what was happening. Julie hadn't contacted him since their meeting, she'd seen no point after his comments as he left her flat. But thankfully she still had his card. Hopefully, they wouldn't need to use it on their mission to find Mandy. If she had spoken to anyone else but Angela, they would simply have questioned her sanity. They wouldn't have believed her, and again there was still no proof that the voice at the end of the phone was even her sister.

Angela was the only one who really believed her. And Julie knew her friend was truly intrigued by Duro. But she could tell she was nervous and felt safer bringing Ned along. Julie felt the same way.

Julie needed to bring Mandy back home despite feeling nauseous and full of trepidation about the whole thing. The doubts and fears consumed her as she lay in bed, longing for sleep. She told herself that whatever happened, when she returned home, with or without her sister, that she would never return to Duro again.

The plan seemed perfect, almost too perfect. Ned turned up a day early.

"I'm feeling eager and energetic," he giggled, smiling widely. He embraced Angela in a warm hug, kissing her cheek. He turned towards Julie and said, "so..., you must be the mysterious Julie?"

Julie liked him instantly and asked why Angela had never introduced her to him before.

Laughing, Angela replied. "I know right, but trying to pin him down is hard enough, I never know where he is, or what he's been up to, and I don't think I could forgive myself if he broke your heart."

Angela had mentioned on a few occasions that Ned wasn't ever serious about anyone; he was a free spirit and when women had come along and tried to tame him, he'd always go AWOL. Many an evening she would be on the phone listening to another heartbroken soul.

"But…" she would hear them cry. "He told me he loved me."

She could only sigh and apologise for his ways.

So, when meeting Ned, Julie understood how anyone could fall for him. The energy, humour, the boyish ways, his cheeky smile, and mid-length brown curls. She could see him as a pirate or a Romany gypsy, his skin heavily tanned from working outside, she could understand that he'd be easy to fall in love with. The beauty of it was that when you got to know him, he wasn't arrogant or full of himself, he was just the sweetest person, with the kindest of hearts, and she couldn't keep up with the amount of tea he drank.

They sat looking at the secret map of the underground mazes

Julie had lost count of how many pots of tea she'd made. She didn't mind because for the first time in a long time she felt comfortable, and safe.

"Now," Ned said suddenly, all business like, "tell me the whole story, don't leave anything out." So, Julie told him everything, finishing with the call from someone that she thought was Mandy pleading for help.

He whistled between his teeth. "Geez, I guess we gotta bring your sister back, it sounds like your Ma needs rescuing too."

"Thank you." She almost whispered, truly believing he would. She'd only known Ned a day, but already felt she could rely totally on him.

They stayed up most of the night, plotting, planning, drinking, and eating…, and laughing. It was almost a new emotion for Julie. She'd forgotten how much she liked it.

Talking to Angela in the kitchen, after another drink break, she said, "I'm so glad Ned came up early. There is so much more to plan than I realised. Be honest, have you been thinking the same thing?"

Angela nodded, almost sheepishly. "I actually thought it could be that easy. But, talking to Ned, I know it won't, it can't be, Jules. We just need a plan B. That's one thing Ned's really good at. See you tomorrow, Jules." She gave her a peck on her cheek as she always did. Julie heard the door close behind them. Already feeling alone again.

Julie awoke to a knocking on the door and heard Ned calling through the letterbox.

"Hey, sleepy head, breakfast is being served."

"Okay." She replied, grabbing a black sweatshirt and throwing it over her long black cotton nighty. Taking a quick look in the mirror at her short urchin cut, which she still couldn't get used to, and picking up her house keys she went to Angela's.

"Hey," smiled her friend, warmly. The smell of percolated coffee wafting across the room.

"Mmm, you know me so well, fresh coffee in the morning." Julie smiled back.

"Ned's already on his second pot of tea," Angela laughed. They sat at Angela's heavy glass dining room table on grey velour, high-backed chairs.

Ned had filled bagels with salmon and cream cheese and was tucking in heartedly.

"Morning Jules," he said in a way that made her feel as if she'd known him for years. It was a good, welcome feeling.

He had made a dozen copies of the Duro map showing its mazes.

"These maps I've printed off are spares, to hand out, if need be, and I have taken a photo on my mobile which I think we should all have."

"I would never have thought of that." Julie replied, taking a slurp of her coffee.

"That's because you are emotionally involved." Smiled Ned. "But I've studied the map and although I think we will find your sister and maybe even Susan, we may also be putting ourselves in danger, so we need to get this right."

After breakfast, Angela telephoned The Gateway enquiring if there was any bar work available., explaining they had previous experience from when they were at university. Luckily, they were looking for staff as a couple of their staff had recently left. She glanced over at Julie and Ned and gave them a thumbs up. Angela asked when they could start.

"Yes, Friday is perfect! Thank you." Angela ended the call.

She turned to look at them. "We start on Friday evening," she said, beaming. "We need to be there at 10am so they can show us the ropes."

"I so want to find my sister," Julie said absently, reaching across the table for another bagel. "But. I'm absolutely terrified."

"It seems strange that The Gateway are needing more staff, no-one seems to stay very long?" Queried Angela. "I wonder what's happening to them, or why they don't seem to stay around?"

Julie dreaded the thought of coming face to face with Aunty, Paul or Jack ever again. Angela and Ned said they would take the lead.

They didn't need to leave for Duro for another two days. Julie decided to go for an even shorter haircut, have her eyebrows tinted darker with a thicker shape that gave a defined look, and her lips plumped, hoping she bore no resemblance to the person who had previously visited this hidden hamlet of secrets.

Ned decided they should leave late afternoon. Angela and Julie had packed most things to go in the campervan. He laughed when he saw the contents.

"You really don't need any of this stuff," he chuckled. "I don't store, I only buy what I need. There are shops we can stop at." He smiled.

Angela and Julie hadn't even seen the campervan yet and were slightly anxious about what it would look like inside and the sleeping arrangements.

"By the way," Ned said, looking over at Julie. "You look great."

Julie couldn't help but smile.

"Thanks," she replied shyly.

Angela loved the look too.

"Oh wow!" She spoke. "You look so different, but in a great way. Let's hope your sister recognises you, when we find her."

Julie smiled but felt so jittery.

Repacking with light luggage this time, they locked up their apartments, not quite sure what would be in store and when they would be returning.

Walking to the car park, both stopped and gasped.

"What's up, Laydees?" Asked Ned, his green eyes surrounded by thick black eyelashes dancing with his smile.

"Did you think I lived in a pokey shack on wheels?" Ned laughed, sarcastically. "Shame on your street cred about me."

"Really?" cried out Angela. "You kept this quiet; I would have thought you would have upgraded by now; you have had this old banger for years!"

"You like it then sis?" He laughed, "it is an old Bedford, and a Rascal, at that." It was white in colour with a dirty yellow bonnet.

"I certainly didn't think I would be travelling to Duro in such luxury, and I can't wait to see inside this beautiful looking vehicle." Julie smirked. But she was horrified.

"Your carriage awaits," said Ned as he opened the vehicle's door, that had definitely seen better days.

Stepping inside the faint smell wafted subtle undertones of pears soap and sandalwood, giving a lovely aroma, which made up for his worn and torn interior and all surfaces covered in a cheap walnut looking Formica.

Gingerly sitting on a thin, faded orange foam seat, Angela shifted trying to get comfortable for the long journey ahead.

"Your last motorhome was lovely." said Angela, bemused.

"Well, I had to sell it, I needed the cash. My mate sold me this little beauty for a job I did to help him out. It had to be done." He replied as he unpacked milk, butter and cheese into the small fridge. Even the fridge door was covered in cheap walnut Formica.

He put the address into the sat nav as Angela and Julie put on their seatbelts.

"Has my sister told you about the life that I love to live? On the road stopping off here and there getting to know people and doing odd jobs."

"Sounds perfect." Julie dreamily replied, "it must be so exhilarating to be able to be that free. I envy you."

Ned started the engine. The Rascal rattled. Julie wasn't convinced it was going to make the journey.

"There is no going back! Let's do this thing. Road trip!" Ned laughed. "This Rascal has got plenty of life in it yet."

Julie wasn't so sure; she was secretly terrified and felt a lump of anxiety rise in her throat. Making sure no-one was looking; she popped a pill.

TWELVE

Julie jumped awake to the sound of Ned screaming, bolting upright as Angela gripped her arm so hard it hurt.

"I think it's one of them!" she screamed and whispered in fear. Even in the dark, Julie could see her eyes were filled with absolute terror.

"What?" Julie was trying to work out where she was, still half-asleep, but alert to Ned's screams. People like Ned didn't scream. In her befuddled mind she wasn't sure exactly what was happening, but she knew something was very wrong. She must have slept through the whole journey.

Her eyes adjusted slowly to the darkness, she saw they were parked up at the jetty in Duro. And suddenly, there it was, a Watcher! Her heart stopped and she started to shake uncontrollably. This was something she had hoped to never see again.

"You saw it didn't you?" said Angela, still holding her arm. She could hear Ned breathing., but barely saw him in the dull light. He was laughing, but she knew that wasn't a Ned laugh. He was sweating, and crying, and his face was ashen.

Seemingly talking to himself, he said, quietly. "So horrible, just a blank face staring in the window. I knew what it was, but I didn't really believe it. Didn't make me jump exactly, it was just there when I looked outside," said Ned. "As soon as it saw me looking back at it, it just seemed to disappear. Like it just vanished back into the marshes. That is the single most frightening thing that has ever happened to me. Can I have a cup of tea, please…, and can we close the curtains?"

"Horrible creepy-looking black figures." Ned went on, "almost demon-like. They made me scream, and I'm not usually scared of anything, it was like it was looking straight through me, sinister and faceless." He shuddered.

In silence they sat and sipped their tea and ate biscuits, hoping they were safe in the Rascal. The windows and doors were locked, and although the van had tinted windows, they were all glad they had decided to close the curtains.

"I'm sleeping in my clothes tonight," said Ned randomly. "Just in case, although…." he added, "there must be a good fifty people staying in this car park tonight, we can't be the only ones who saw that thing!"

It was a sobering thought but still not welcoming in any way, knowing these creatures were skulking around out there.

Thankfully, Thursday morning finally arrived. After having a restless night and sleeping on a thin, worn foam mattress which had seen better days. Ned was up early and making breakfast in the Rascal. As they ate, they discussed how to spend the day,

before putting their plan of action into place. Angela was keen to take a trip out to Duro Rock, Julie agreed as long as it wasn't on a boat called *'Jackie'*. Angela glanced at her but said nothing.

The weather was humid but cloudy and there were a few people in the car park milling about wondering whether to take umbrellas.

"A Pac a Mac will do us." said Ned, eagerly. "C'mon, chop chop, let's beat the crowds." He was back to his normal devil-may-care self.

Julie looked worriedly up and down the river to see if she could spot Jack or Paul, but the coast was clear.

They saw a small boat, with the name *'Amanda'*, which immediately caught Julie's attention. Angela obviously saw it too and touched her arm. She smiled at Julies, "a good omen?"

They boarded the bright green vessel.

"Ahoy, my matey's," smiled the captain, looking no older than twelve years old, his weather-beaten face covered in freckles and twinkly brown eyes peering out from under a tweed cloth hat.

"And who may I ask, do I have the pleasure of welcoming aboard my lovely *'Amanda*?"

Ned smiled, shaking the lad's hand.

"Ned," he replied. "This is Emma and Anna. We came down last night and thought we would spend a day over the rock before these two lovelies start work at The Gateway. Tomorrow."

"Nice one, I'm Tim," the lad smiled, shaking Ned's hand warmly, "I promise, you won't regret it, it really is something to see."

"If you need any help or backup, I'm about." said Ned, jokingly.

Tim nodded, "good to know," he grinned. They seemed to have bonded almost immediately.

Journeying up the river, Julie looked over towards Ma's. I wonder where you are Mandy. She thought. Are you at the Pastures? On the rock somewhere? Or being 'looked after' by Aunty at The Post Office? Just the mere thought made her blood run cold.

"Penny for your thoughts, Emma?" asked Tim, smiling down at her. Much as she'd taken a liking to him, Julie certainly wasn't going to tell him or anyone else about her actual thoughts.

She simply grinned back "They're not worth a penny, Tim," she laughed. "Just taking in the scenery, it's so serene and peaceful here. There's a word that keeps popping into my mind…, idyllic."

"If only you knew." Tim looked at her and chuckled, quietly.

Ned immediately seemed to pick up on this. "What do you mean, know what?"

"Just strange doings," Tim answered nervously, as he looked around. "No-one is supposed to talk about it. The Watchers and The Listeners are about. They've always been here. We're told they guard Duro. They're terrifying." He finished quietly.

Ned nodded earnestly in response.

"Yes, we saw a black shape in the darkness last night. Scared the hell out of all of us. Have you seen one?"

It took Tim a long while to answer. It was obvious that he was contemplating whether he should answer or try to laugh it off.

Finally, he said."Yes, I saw a Watcher once, when I was a young lad."

"So, what are they?" Ned pressed the point gently. "I've never seen or felt anything like it. Just nothing, and the dread, the sheer emptiness of that non-existent gaze."

Looking at Ned, sighing deeply, and resignedly, Tim continued. "The Watchers only seem to come out at night. It's almost like they're looking for something or someone. They're just checking everyone who comes here. Almost like passport control. We've always been told they live in the Marshes. It's a small village, and everyone knows that people have disappeared around the jetty, although they'd never admit it. Apparently, they were so terrified and transfixed by the black figures they'd let themselves be dragged into the river. Never to be seen again."

Everyone was silent and no more was mentioned about The Watchers. The boat chopped through the calm waters of the bay, the Rock coming steadily closer.

Angela, who had been strangely quiet for most of the day, suddenly said, "And what about The Listeners, Tim?"

Tim looked at her sharply, "no one knows much about The Listeners, I don't think they want to. Maybe some of the older villagers might, but you don't want to go asking them. They'll tell you nothing, and you'll just get noticed, and here, that's something you really don't need. Although I guess you're here for more than just a holiday?" Tim said nothing for the rest of the journey.

It was a creepy thought and after hearing it, Julie was not sure if she was strong enough for this. She'd mention it later to Angela and Ned, perhaps if they could at least find Mandy, they could call the police and let them do the rest. Julie knew it was a selfish thought and was ashamed of herself.

The boat headed out to the delta along with other vessels heading towards Duro Rock, as Tim turned the boat and started to head towards the base of The Rock. This time the beauty of The Rock hit Julie. She noticed more scenery this time around, suspecting that Mandy might still be alive, the trip was surprisingly relaxing. The pink marble of the hotel, the old monks' abbey shimmered even more so in the sunlight and this time she was with friends. They looked at the stunning building, there was so much to take in.

"I could lose myself here," smiled Angela.

"Who does the old farmhouse belong to?" Asked Ned, pointing in the near distance to the right of The Rock, knowing too well it belonged to Julie's grandma.

Tim cleared his throat and looked at Ned.

"You wanna stay away from there, Ned," he replied, sharply. "That's ol' Ma Saltern's place. She owns all the right side of The Pastures. Folks tend to stay away from there. Villagers say she is a dabbler in witchcraft, a Wicca."

Ned pretended to play dumb, "what is a Wicca? Sorry, mate, I'm a city boy, I've travelled about a bit, but never heard of that before." He seemed to have a bond with Tim, although they'd only known each for a few hours.

"A witch!" Tim said simply. He didn't look at Ned as he said this. Ned decided to leave it, for now, at least.

As Tim moored up *Amanda*, Ned asked if he would pick them up later and take them back to The Gateway.

Tim nodded, "Of course, it's all part of the service," he grinned, seemingly more comfortable with the conversation.

As Julie and Angela stood at the mooring, Ned leaned over to Tim.

"Listen, mate, I know this is something you clearly don't want, or can't talk about, but who are The Listeners? we really need to know."

Tim shrugged his shoulders, "sorry Ned, I really can't tell you anything more than I've told you already. I've probably already said too much, I'll meet you all here back at four, Ok with you?"

"Works for us," Ned said, easily.

Turning his back, and stepping back on his boat, he moved away from the jetty and steered off.

"See you at four." he shouted, not looking back.

Ned nodded in reply and turned away dejectedly. He couldn't, and wouldn't say anything to Julie and Angela, that would only make a fragile situation worse. But what Tim had said to him about making things even more difficult, the thought disturbed him a lot. Deep inside, he truly hoped he would see Tim at four o'clock. The thought that maybe just talking to him and asking questions had put him in danger.

"Well?" Asked Ned, "and what did we all make of *that* conversation?" He was trying to sound nonchalant, but it was easy to see that was far from what he was really feeling.

Finally swallowing her doubt, Julie said, "I think we should find out where Mandy is… inform the police and then make our way home."

For the first time since she'd met Ned, the look he gave her had no sign of warmth. Angela was staring at her, looking like she didn't know her anymore. Ned's response was emphatic, almost cold.

"When we find Mandy, Jules, could you really leave her here, especially after all *you* went through yourself!? I mean seriously?" Ned was defiant, almost angry, something that Julie had never seen in him before.

"Mandy will be coming back with us, or not at all! Do you really want the local police dealing with this? Half of them are villagers. If there really is something going on here, which there clearly is, how hard and deep do you think they'll investigate? Let's keep Duro quiet."

Walking up the spiral pathway in an uncomfortable silence, which Julie knew was her fault, the courtyard opened up to the square of shops. The red and white striped awnings, the round silver tables and chairs were so inviting to stop for coffee.

"Right," he said, clapping his hands, "cappuccinos all around." It immediately broke the tension between them. Ned and Angela were clearly enjoying the moment. Drinking coffee while taking in the number of tourists mulling around.

Speaking quietly, she said sheepishly, "I'm so sorry about earlier. I lost it there for a moment, thinking I couldn't do what we came here to do. I'm just so scared."

Angela said sharply, but warmly, "Jules, we're all terrified, I know I am. And as for Ned? I know he is, too, the bravado is just his way of dealing with it. I absolutely know that inside her feels exactly the same as us." She smiled at Julie, held her arm, and suddenly everything was back in perspective.

"Well, let's go and have a look at the Monastery." Ned said loudly, "that's all we really came here for."

"Keep your eyes and ears open for any info," Julie whispered.

"Look out for people in the area listening to any of our conversations." said Ned, quietly... "and also for anyone who might be watching us," he grinned. It was supposed to be funny, something to lighten the mood. It didn't work for Julie…, her blood ran cold.

"For such a small hidden place," observed Angela. "It's crammed with tourists."

"I can't get my head around how busy it is," said Ned. "If it's always like this how come staff come and go from The

Gateway so often. On a day like this, they must be making a fortune."

Angela looked at Ned and started making ghostly noises. "Maybe they are turned into one of The Watchers whose souls are turned into creatures of the dark," she taunted. Julie knew that Angela was joking, but to her it was no laughing matter.

"Stop it!" Julie said sharply, trying to keep the edge from her voice, and make the comment sound light-hearted. "Don't forget, my friend, that this time tomorrow, we'll both be working at The Gateway. I don't really want to think about why the staff turnover is so high."

"And," Ned butted in, "we'll all be going there, and I'll be walking back with you once you have finished your shifts. Neither of you will be left alone. I'll make sure of that." Again, he gave that reassuring smile.

Julie was so grateful Ned was here. She really wasn't looking forward to working behind the bar at The Gateway, though. She was completely out of her comfort zone, having no idea what to expect or even imagine what could happen.

As Angela and Julie were finishing their coffees Ned decided to casually take a look in Ma's shop returning later with a large jar of honey.

"What an amazing shop, all the tinctures too, and all available in brown glass bottles," he said. "Absolutely astonishing! It's like going back a hundred years." He placed the octagonal-shaped jar of golden honey on the table, along with a brown bottle tincture of arnica. "You say that she makes everything here?" He asked.

Julie nodded "Yes, I think so, that's what I've heard, anyway, let's go to the top of The Rock, and check out the Monastery. We can see across to The Pastures and watch the workers at Ma's then go to the chapel, which I missed out on last time."

Leaving a tip, they walked up the path towards the Monastery. Ned took absolutely no interest in the new hotel, with its huge white balls of macrophylla hydrangea which stood out strikingly against the rolled green lawn. In front, the roaring stone lions, which were once the entrance to the Monks living quarters.

Once inside, the coolness was pleasing from the heat outside. The day was humid, it was an unpleasant, sticky warmth. The same woman was sitting at a reception desk, this time she wasn't on the telephone but was using an emery board on her long red painted fingernails.

She looked up as they walked past, taking a second glance at Ned. It seemed to Julie that she did a double take when she saw her. It was disconcerting, she didn't look anything like when she'd been here before.

"Good morning, can I help?" She asked, smiling broadly, but emptily, with lips painted the same red as her nail varnish.

"Nah, we're good, thanks," replied Ned, giving his best smile, "we're just having a look around." He beamed.

As Angela walked past the receptionist, she looked over. "If you need anything, just let me know. I'm Alison, by the way. We want you to enjoy your visit at The Monastery." A plastic smile, clearly scripted dialogue. Angela slowly began to understand, they couldn't trust anyone.

The vast rounded library had changed slightly, and another chaise lounge had been added adjacent to the blue velvet one of the same colour. The heavy glass paned doors were wide open with a scent wafting over from the deep pinked dog rose intertwined with white delicate flowers of syringa. It was heavenly.

Ned walked directly to the telescope with his one-pound coin at the ready. Julie hoped he didn't notice her staring but with his eye looking through the scope he could have easily passed as a swashbuckling buccaneer.

He put another one-pound coin into the slot and carried on peering through the viewfinder for what seemed to be an eternity.

"What do you see?" Angela asked.

Ned didn't really answer her question, "I could stand and watch through this viewer all day," Ned replied. He had been distracted by the workers over at Ma's with their blue headscarves and long blue dresses and with white aprons. "You can see the beehives, and the workers pruning and picking different herbs. It's fascinating, and addictive to watch."

Julie nodded, and smiled over at Angela, it was like watching a small boy.

"Let me have a look, as I would like to see!"
Said Angela getting up from the comfort of the chair.

They finished spending most of their change on the telescope then amiably strolled around the garden and building absorbing the wondrous sights surrounding them. Making their way to the chapel taking in the glorious rhododendron bushes out in full pink blooms.

The chapel door was open, and Julie was speechless. The sunlight shining through the stained-glass windows looked like rainbows of bright colours dancing on the walls. The golden pews and the carvings were a sight to behold.

"Right," said Ned, looking at his watch, "we better get back down to meet Tim, it's nearly four."

Ned was distracted as they walked down towards the mooring. He was hoping it actually was Tim that they'd be meeting. His earlier thoughts had been nagging at him all day.

As they drew closer to the water, Ned could see the *'Amanda',* bobbing gaily at the mooring. His heart sank, and his body went cold. He could see, even from this distance, that it wasn't Tim standing on the deck.

Ned approached the boat, and said as light-heartedly as he could manage.

"Hello. You're not Tim."

"Very perceptive," the guy laughed, easily, "no, I'm his better-looking brother, Andy," he grinned, "Did you enjoy your day on The Rock?"

"I could stay here forever." replied Ned, absently, "so, where is Tim, then?"

"I'm not certain to be honest. I got a call from him a couple of hours ago, saying he had to go 'somewhere', but didn't say where, mind you. Normally, he'd give me too many details, but not today. Strange for him," he looked slightly perturbed, "but we both look after *'Amanda'*, so he asked me to make sure I was here at four to pick you lovely people up. So here I am, if you're ready, step aboard m'hearties."

Despite the dark feelings clouding his thoughts, Ned couldn't find anything not to like about Andy. Friendly, affable, and clearly with a good sense of humour. Ned considered himself a good judge of character and could tell that Andy was his kind of person. On a more selfish note, they might be able to get a few more answers.

Julie and Angela finally reached the boat.

"Where's Tim?" Julie asked, tightly, looking directly at Ned, real concern in her eyes. Angela also looked disconcerted.

"Nothing to worry about, Tim got called away urgently. This is Andy, he's come to take us back to The Gateway, he works with Tim, so, at least we know we won't be sleeping on The Rock tonight." He tried his best to smile, but both Julie and Angela knew it wasn't a 'real' Ned smile.

"Good afternoon, my fair ladies," said Andy, appearing from the front of the boat. He doffed his cap charmingly, "I'm sorry to say that young Tim has been called away on an urgent errand. You'll have to settle for the better-looking younger brother."

The chat on the way back to The Gateway, was affable, but non-committal. Still, Ned was determined to try.

"The telescope thing at The Monastery is amazing," he said, simply standing next to Andy.

"Yes, I still go up there myself sometimes, when I'm waiting for people. I tell you, Ned, I've lived here all my life, and the view, although it's the same, it's always different."

He looked over at Ned, "Does that make sense?" He seemed genuinely interested in Ned's response.

"Complete sense," he replied, smiling genuinely, "I find the same with the Lake District. No matter how many times I go, usually to the same places, the view might be the same, but the feelings are always different. Except what I'm looking at, nothing is ever the same. But it's always breathtaking."

"Yeah," Andy said simply.

"Nothing better. Tops up your soul."

There was a comfortable silence between them. And neither of them spoke for a while. As Andy navigated around the headland, The Gateway loomed into view. Ned looked back at Julie and Angela, they were laughing and obviously involved in their own conversation, oblivious to anything else. Maybe a good thing. He decided to go for it.

"Andy?"

"Yes, my friend?"

"Can I ask you a question?"

"Sure, of course, and if I can, I might actually be able to answer it." He was trying to keep things upbeat.

"What's the whole farming thing going on over there," Ned pointed vaguely to the right, "looks like a real hive of activity. And they're all dressed the same?" He deliberately made a question that had to be answered.

"Oh, that's Ma's place. The Pastures they call it. We never see Ma. Not sure I'd really want to, to be honest. From what I know, that's where she makes all her pills, potions and tinctures to sell locally. Don't understand it, so keep myself well out of it. Although, I know Tim met her once. When he returned home, he wasn't the same for a couple of days. Then, he seemed to slowly come back to himself. I'm sure you and your friends have already worked out that Duro is a bit..., different, and perhaps, not in a good way." He looked across good-naturedly at Ned. "Just be careful, mate. Seriously, you really don't know who you can trust, so trust no-one, because everyone will be watching you."

"And here we are, safely back at The Gateway," he shouted loudly, "go eat, drink and be merry." He winked surreptitiously at Ned as he got off the boat.

"I hope you find what you're looking for. If you need me, I'm about most days, someone will be able to find me." They shook hands.

"Say hello and thanks to Tim when you see him." Ned said, sincerely.

Andy looked at him, and replied. "I will…, if I can.."
Returning to the Rascal they reminisced on the day's events as they sat and ate jam sandwiches, and fruitcake. Obviously with a big pot of tea. Ned sat back and sighed as he took his first mouthful. "Now, that is nectar," he grinned.

Julie could tell Ned was in deep thought, so she asked him what he was thinking.

"Well, when I was looking through the viewfinder I looked across from The Rock to The Pastures, those underground passages must be very deep and very long…., and I'm wondering about Tim," he said distractedly.

"Why?" asked Angela, "I thought Andy said he'd been called away on an urgent bit of business?"

"It's just what he said as he was about to head back to The Gateway," Ned paused, "I asked him about The Listeners again, but he said he'd probably already said too much. He didn't look scared exactly, more…, I don't know, resigned. It's been playing on my mind all day. I can't get the thought out of my head that I pushed him too far. I kept asking him questions that he was clearly uncomfortable answering."

"But I thought it sounded like you were just showing an interest," said Angela, "try not to overthink things, Ned."

"Hmm." But both Julie and Angela could tell he wasn't convinced.

Having heard what Ned said about the tunnels, Julie was even more fearful. Her heart went cold. But knew somehow, she'd had to brave the tunnels if she wanted to find her sister. Although she wasn't sure how she would react if she came face to face with anything she couldn't deal with. She'd be totally alone, but even knowing her friends were somewhere above her, waiting, ready to raise the alarm if she didn't return, the thought was comforting, but wasn't going to help her if a situation did arise, and things went wrong.

It was Friday morning. Julie and Angela were getting ready for their induction at The Gateway. Ned had assured them he would be sitting in the bar the whole time they were working and would be aware of anything suspicious. If either of them felt they were in any danger or any concerns they would start coughing to attract attention and no one would be any the wiser.

"Cool with that idea?" He asked, looking at them both earnestly, "seriously, we've got our plan, but with the best will in the world, we'll just have to see how things actually pan out. Once we have a better idea, we can make changes. Just try and find out as much as you can when you're in there. I'm just going to wave, and wish you 'good luck' as you walk over there, ok?"

"Good with this?" Said Angela as they walked across the car park towards The Gateway.

"No," Julie replied tightly, "I've never been less sure of anything in my whole life." As she glanced back over at Angela. They smiled. Such a simple gesture seemed to lift the mood, but only slightly. Neither really knew what was going to happen next.

They continued to walk towards the seventeenth-century tavern. The bleached wood decking supporting picnic benches facing the ferry boats on the River Duro. The hanging baskets of colour, the trailing blue aubretia, the pretty creeping Jenny and the red trailing fuchsia made for a welcoming entrance.

"OK girl," said Angela, "Game faces on." She gripped Julie's arm for a second.

"Good morning, welcome to The Gateway. I'm Debs, and you must be Emma and Anna?" They nodded, smiling back.

"Yep, that's us," answered Angela, brightly.

Debs was so tiny, her skinny black jeans, black vest and white trainers, a casual look which suited her. Her face had a natural prettiness.

"Come with me, let me just show you what it's all about. I know you've got previous experience, and you can't unlearn what you learn at Uni, Can you?" She said laughing. It was annoying, she was so easy to like. But both of them knew, they had to be on their guard.

They followed her meekly, like sheep as she explained what would be expected of them.

"Oh." She said, suddenly turning around, her long blonde ponytail following. "I almost forgot, your rooms are already made up for your stay… they come free, one of the perks of the job."

"We don't need a room, but thanks for the offer." Replied Angela. "We've bought our own campervan. We're on a bit of a road-trip. Early life crisis, I guess. We recently met up with a relative from Uni, he's a bit of a free spirit, so he suggested we tour in the van, and go exploring, and here we are. He's probably sitting outside reading a book." Angela made a great job of sounding exasperated. "But he's exactly the same as I remember him …. annoying, but with a heart of gold."

"Yeah, and being a PA isn't exactly living your best life," Julie chimed in, "always being told what to do, and when it has to be done by. No, thanks."

Despite their pointless babble, they both noticed that Deb's mood seemed to change slightly, at the mention of them not wanting to stay at The Gateway.

"Mr. Salterns expects that employees stay here at the tavern." Her voice was still light, but it almost sounded uncomfortably like it was compulsory. "He owns The Gateway and pops in daily and enjoys chatting to the staff."

Julie's heart froze when she heard the name, Salterns. Her surname.

Her family name. Did her dad's brother, an uncle of hers, still own this side of Duro? And if so, where, and who was he? She didn't want these thoughts when they were working on the Mandy plan.

Debs showed them the different drinks and the glasses to use. Noticing the confused looks on their faces, Debs reassured them and told them not to worry, the locals would always step in and help if they were stuck with anything, especially if they thought they might get a free drink out of it.

"If you get low on stock or need to change the barrels, this is where you go, just follow me. I hope that's o.k,unless you need to know anything else on this side of the bar?" Debs didn't even wait to hear a response, "No? Cool. Right, now I'll show you the cellar. Not everyone's favourite place, although I quite like it down there, it lets me think." As if coming out of a dream, she smiled back at them, "it's just quiet, you know? Sometimes you just need that, to try and remember who you really are." Debs smiled; Julie thought it was a sad smile and couldn't help wondering why.

Ned had said not to question anything they were told, as they didn't want to cause any suspicion, or draw attention to themselves. Duro had had enough questions about the two girls, who went missing. Whatever was going on here was carefully hidden. They were here to find Mandy, end of story. And for that, they needed to try and remain anonymous. "Keep well under the radar," was one of Ned's favourite sayings, "it's always worked for me."

On the way Julie noticed the telephone had gone.

As they followed Debs through the bar to the cellar door, Julie realised the thread she found from Mandy's garment proved her sister had definitely been taken through this doorway. Debs opened the latch and took them down some very modern stairs into the cellar. They were totally out of character with the rest of The Gateway.

Debs noticed their puzzled looks.

"Yes, we had to put sturdier stairs in as it's such an old building, the original ones had started to rot. Health and Safety. You know what they're like." She lifted her eyes towards the ceiling, and gave an exasperated sigh, "now we have to look at that eyesore every time we come down here."

They both nodded.

"Yes, they certainly spoil the aesthetics of the place," said Angela.

They weren't sure what they expected to see in the cellar, but whatever it was, it certainly wasn't what they actually saw. There were bottles, cans and barrels of beer. That was it. Julie's heart dropped. Nothing looked like it was obstructing a door, and the room looked so much smaller than she'd imagined it would be.

"Ok," Debs said as they ascended to the bar again. Julie noticed the latch was heavily padlocked. Debs must have seen her looking as she locked it.

"Oh," She laughed, "the padlock is in place to stop people going down there to steal our stock. Any questions?" She asked.

"Nope, I don't think so?" answered Angela, brightly, "oh just one, who do we ask for the key if we need to go down there to restock? I'd hate to be stuck with a bunch of thirsty punters and no beer." She grinned easily at Debs. Julie was amazed at how good she was at becoming another person and slipping into another skin.

"There will always be someone around to open up if you need to go down there."

They didn't have a chance to reply.

"Great," smiled Debs. "See you later, then. Your shifts will be five to ten-thirty. But Mr Salterns will want to meet you, and he'll like to know why you won't stay here."

"No problem," said Angela, indifferently, "we'll look forward to meeting him. See you at five, then. Thanks for your time, Debs."

They saw Ned, who was sitting on the bank of the river reading a book. As he saw them walking towards him, he lifted his hand in greeting. He cheekily grinned his boyish, charming smile.

"Hello, ladies, and how was work?"

"Not as rewarding as we hoped," answered Julie, dejectedly.

"OK, someone's a bit grumpy," he said, lightly, but knowing it meant that they hadn't found what they were looking for, "let's turn that frown upside down. Chicken Caesar salad and garlic bread are waiting." He put his arms around their shoulders as they walked back to the Rascal.

They decided to eat lunch outside, again wanting to add to the image of being nothing more than happy campers. They laughed and joked. And in between they filled Ned in on what they'd seen, or more to the point what they'd not seen. Ned wrote everything down on the pad he'd laid by his right leg. Another laugh and a joke.

"So, you never noticed any doors or handles in the cellar?" He asked, quietly. Julie shook her head.

"It was a very small cellar for such a big building, and Debs put a massive padlock on the hatch when we came back up into the bar. I didn't see exactly where she put the key, she just leaned down for a moment, and said the cellar door must always be kept locked, to make sure no-one could break in and steal the stock.

 She must have put the key under the bar when she was leaning down, that's the only place it can be."

"And" butted in Angela. "The stairs are a very recent addition, totally out of character with the rest of the place."

"That doesn't mean anything, unfortunately. What she said about Health and Safety actually makes sense. In fact, it's the only thing about this place that does, just about the only true thing I've heard since we've been here," said Ned. "What I find really strange though, is that she said Mr Salterns expects the staff to stay there…, why? I can't work that out, but it just doesn't feel right."

"I'm feeling very nervous about all of this," Julie said.

"Well," carried on Ned, seeming not to have heard, or simply not listening, "We can't call the police as we have no proof of anything at all. All laugh and joke now. We've been sitting quietly for far too long, we're here on holiday, remember?"

They laughed, not really knowing whether it sounded authentic or not.

After their 'performance', Julie said immediately, "I also noticed the telephone on the bar wasn't there anymore."

No one said anything and made a point of not looking at each other. Silence. They were all deep in thought.

"We really need a key cut of the padlock to the cellar. You said it's kept under the bar? Right?" asked Ned.

Julie and Angela both nodded.

"But how?" Julie asked, feeling anxiety levels rising again, not that she didn't already feel on the edge.

Ned produced a ball of plasticine, "you just need to make an imprint of the key into this, I'll then have a couple of keys cut from the copy. I'll give you both a ball, so we've got two chances."

"I just don't know if I can do this, Ned. How can we get a copy of the key, when there are so many eyes about."

"Sorry Jules, I don't know what to say to you. If you really want to find and save Mandy, you're just going to have to grow a pair, and try. Seriously. We're here to try and help you, but we can't do everything, you need to just step up, sometimes." His voice was hard, a sound she wasn't used to from Ned. She looked across at Angela, but she was staring into her hands. She looked almost embarrassed.

"You know, Jules, you're my best friend, but I think Ned's right."Angela piped up.

"Right, let's just try and keep things calm. Sorry Jules, if I upset you." said Ned, glancing round the car park. "Let's just keep our voices down, we're having a disagreement about what to do between now and your shift. We won't do anything reckless, we must be patient and take our time with this. To think though, that The Gateway is still owned by your family."

Now they had been into the cellar. Ned got the map of the passageways and tunnels out to study again.

"Can either of you work out where in the cellar there could be a door to a passageway?"

But looking on the map, the pathways of the tunnels didn't seem to join up anywhere near The Gateway.

"Maybe there is another cellar?" queried Angela.

"I'm not so sure," replied Ned, pushing his curly hair back off his face. "In the Duro book, it says the monks kept their wares in the passageways from The Gateway Tavern, when it was an old coaching house. Did you notice anything at all? Even a slight indentation in the wall anywhere?"

Angela's eyes brightened. "You know, I didn't check the walls, I was too busy looking for a door. What an idiot." She slapped a hand against her forehead.

"And how about you, Jules?" Ned asked.

"No, like Angela I was fixated on finding that door without seeming too interested. I had a feeling that Debs was always watching us, picking up on facial expressions or things we said. I can see why she's running the place."

There was clearly a lot to think about. There was silence in the Rascal.

"Well, there's one thing I am certain about, I'm not staying at The Gateway ever again! I don't care what Mr Salterns says." Julie said quietly. "The last time I stayed there I was drugged, or that's what Paul's aunt told me. I ordered a latte, and the last thing I clearly remember was it had an aftertaste. I remember waking up with a tender heel, and I struggled to put my foot down to walk."

"What?!" cried out Ned, he put his head in his hands, and sighed, deeply, "why haven't you mentioned this before, Jules?" He was almost, but not quite shouting. "I thought you said this Aunty person was the one who drugged you?"

"Yes, she did, with valerian," Julie replied, alarmed and slightly taken aback by Ned's tone. "But I was first drugged at The Gateway, when I got back from The Rock."

"And Aunty, Paul and Jack, said your life was in danger?" Ned inquired, clearly trying to calm down after hearing her 'revelation'.

Julie nodded in reply.

"Yes, and the woman in Ma's shop on Duro Rock said it too, but I was only told that when I mentioned that I was Mandy's sister, and I was trying to find out what had happened to her."

"I wonder why you were drugged, though?" Ned said, quietly.

"Maybe they thought you'd have something with you?" asked Angela, shrugging her shoulders.

"I can't think what, besides none of my stuff was touched," Julie replied.

"Well," carried on Ned, gravely, "You obviously have something that they want, and they want it enough for your life to be in danger." He looked over at Julie, "we just need to try and figure out what that something is."

"I've always thought it strange that Ma gave my dad and his sister up for adoption, who both died in their thirties. But s**he** kept the other two children. Susan has gone missing along with my sister who both are daughters from the adopted children. I'm related to Ma from an adopted child of hers and my life is in danger!

It also seems every six months staff here just 'move on' without explanation. I just can't work it out, and it's infuriating. There's got to be something!"

Ned stared at Julie, that was quite a speech for her.

"There is something going on in this village, witchcraft or worse." said Ned. "I don't know what. Homemade pharmaceutical properties, really? Then we've also got these weird, almost other-worldly The Watchers, things with no faces and we don't even know who or what The Listeners are." Julie shivered, although it was warm in the Rascal.

"I really don't like it," said Angela, glancing at them both. "I feel so uncomfortable here. In fact, I don't think I've ever felt this uncomfortable in my life. Not ever." There were tears in her eyes, "I've never been so far out of my comfort zone, and we're still not sure if it was actually Mandy that you heard on the phone, asking for help. We don't really know anything, do we? What if the villagers are doing human sacrifices here? Or even some kind of vampirism? Let's leave while we can."

Julie had never seen Angela unravel like this. She was always the strong one. But not now. She moved across to hold her. Angela immediately snuggled in, "I'm sorry, I thought I was strong, but I'm so scared. There's something here that really isn't right. I came to help you and look at me now." She just sobbed into Julie's arms. Julie just held her and let her do what she needed to.

"No." retorted Ned, immediately. "Now we are here, even if you didn't hear your sister on the telephone, which, by the way, I think you did, there is something very wrong going on in this place, and I want to get to the bottom of it. People are being used for something dark and it must be stopped."

And with that Ned started up the Rascal's engine.

"C'mon, let's go shopping. More supplies needed, "I'm nearly out of tea." End of the conversation, Ned was clearly back in control.

As they drove out of the car park, Angela said, bemusedly,

"Ned we've still got plenty of food."

"I know, I just want to be somewhere else for a while, this place stifles me, but more importantly, I want to find somewhere I can get a phone signal. I'm beginning to think we're going to need a bit of help. I just want to make a couple of calls." Julie and Angela looked at each other, puzzled, but said nothing. Ned was obviously clear on what needed to be done.

They drove out of Duro and headed towards the nearest 'town' about twenty miles away. They weren't sure exactly what they would find there, but at least they'd heard of it, and it could be found on a map.

About 15 minutes out of the village, a variety of pings and chimes told them they had a signal. Grinning at each other like small children, they each pulled out their phones. Ned immediately looked for somewhere to pull over. Not bothering to switch off the Rascals engine, they all jumped out.

"Ah, back in the real world. The smell of technology. And ain't it wonderful?" Said Ned laughing and holding his phone up to the sky like he'd just found the Holy Grail.

They spent a few minutes checking their email and texts.

"Isn't it amazing how much rubbish you get?" Said Angela, "I had 47 emails, and 14 texts, and all of them were absolutely pointless." She noticed that Ned and Julie were staring at her, both looking amused. "Sorry," she chuckled, her cheeks flushed, "it's just one of my pet peeves. I'm just going to phone our parents, Ned, to let them know we're still alive…, well, for now, at least." She smiled ironically.

Then Ned moved away to make his calls.

"Hi, Bill, how are you, mate? It's Ned. Listen, buddy, I'm into something down here in Duro. Could any of the boys use a holiday?"

Angela walked back, "yeah, bye Mum…, love you. Speak soon."

Julie had spoken to no-one. She had no-one to speak to. She sat in the Rascal, feeling totally alone, despite being with her friends.

Ned walked over, looking pleased with himself.

"Right, gotta few mates coming down. They should be here early tomorrow. They decided a few days away was just the thing. Don't worry, you'll know when they arrive."

"Oh, Ned, they're not going to antagonise the villagers, are they?" Angela asked, looking worried.

"I kid you not, Sis, they are the nicest bunch of people you'll ever meet. When they get here, I'm going to show them the map, then during the day, they'll go out 'exploring' the local area, based on what we think we know, and what's on the map. Covert Ops is what they call it in the movies. So, they'll be out looking around during the day, and in the evening, they'll be sitting in The Gateway, having a few beers, just lads on holiday, but they'll be keeping an eye on you two. I hope that works for you?" They both nodded eagerly. Anything to make them feel safer. "They'll be there immediately, if anything seems untoward. Believe me, they'll know if anything's not right. And by the way, you're going to love 'em. Just a great bunch of people, and more to the point, you can actually trust them, which makes a nice change in this place."

"Sounds good," said Julie, "Anything to make me feel less nervous."

"Works for me, too," said Angela emphatically.

They both breathed a sigh of relief, although they tried to hide it.

"Thanks, Ned," said Julie, and gave him a peck on the cheek.

They filled up the fridge in the Rascal with milk, eggs and more cheese. And, of course, tea.

With sinking hearts, they headed back to Duro. They'd escaped briefly back into the real world allowing them to breathe again. Now it felt like they were diving back into darkness. No-one spoke on the drive back to The Gateway. Sitting on the faded orange seat, Ned started to explain how he thought their plan needed work to ensure they could rescue Mandy and anyone else held against their will.

"I don't care what you say, I'm convinced that Susan and Mandy are not the only ones in trouble. So, when you go into work this evening the first chance you get to restock up on something, I don't care what, dry peanuts, or whatever these people like. Then just check around again it seems like we've missed something. Maybe run your fingers around the skirting boards, surely the door we are looking for must be fairly noticeable." Julie and Angela nodded, without saying anything.

"The lads are going to scour over the map too, when they arrive, and visit The Rock to try and find out any information." His smile was simple.

"And, even better, they'll be camping just over there." He inclined his head slightly, nodding towards the picnic area.

"What we really need is to get a copy of that key for that padlock," said Ned, "That's priority No 1."

Angela and Julie nodded, and hoped that Neds' mates would be arriving before they started work, but both thought that that was unrealistic. Ned had only called them a few hours ago. They knew they were on their way. Just tonight's shift to get through. Julie needn't have worried though, they arrived just a few hours after Ned had asked the favour. When Angela and Julie were on their shift, they heard and felt the sound of bikes from inside of the tavern. Ten of them roared up to the front of The Gateway.
Bill looked earnestly at the group.

"Remember, we know no-one. I've never been here before, but I've already got a bad feeling about this place. So, polite chat only in front of strangers. We're just down here getting away from everything for a few days." he grinned, "Trust me, after Ned's phone call I feel there could be something very wrong going on here, believe me. So, best behaviour, I'm going to speak to Ned in the morning and to take a look at the map he has spoken about. Right Anyone fancy a pint?"

Angela and Julie made their way to The Gateway to start their first shift., Ned walked over with them, book in hand.

"Think I'll treat myself to a pint, while I watch you work. It's so satisfying watching others work, when you don't have to." He looked at them out of the corner of his eye.

"What are you reading, anyway?" asked Angela.

"It's a bit of a love story, really. *American Psycho*, by Brett Easton Ellis. I think it's quite an apt read for this place." He looked at her, ironically.

"Evening, Debs," Angela said, smiling as they walked in, "well, here we are and ready for action."

Debs smiled over at them, "here in plenty of time, I see. Excellent."

"And this is Ned, who I told you about, who managed to persuade us to get away from reality for a while. He suddenly decided he wanted a drink, and to read his book, while he watches us work."

"Hi, Ned and welcome to The Gateway. I hope you're enjoying your stay?" Julie could have sworn she was blushing slightly, "what can I get you?"

"Hello Debs," giving her a disarming smile, "is it ok to call you Debs? Well, enjoying it, so far. I love The Rock, a great place to visit." He smiled again, "can I have a pint of lager, please?"

"Of course, you go and sit down, I'll bring it over for you." Julie and Angela exchanged an amused glance.

It was relatively quiet, and they realised the daytime shift was likely to be the busiest time, with visitors coming to see Duro Rock and use the ferries. Julie guessed this time of the day visitors would have left by now.

Julie noticed the elderly man who she had seen on her last visit, who'd told her about the phone being used and The Listeners who carried messages on the breeze through the trees. He was sitting at one of the tables engrossed in reading a newspaper, the same as last time she saw him.

Debs pointed him out.

"That's the old man Salterns who I was telling you about. I explained you were just travelling through Duro in your campervan and needed a week or two of work so didn't need a room here."

"Oh," Julie replied, hoping he didn't want to see her or Angela, as she didn't want to be recognised.

"Don't worry," Debs smiled. "He is ok with it, I think it's just he likes to feel that everyone feels like part of a family, quite sweet really." The look Debs gave the old man was almost reverential.

Julie felt a massive weight lift from her shoulders. Debs had called him old man Salturns. She couldn't help but wonder how he was related to her. It certainly wouldn't be her grandpa, this man looked far too young, and Paul's aunt had said she'd not seen her grandfather since he and Ma were married.

"Oh, thanks, Debs, that's been worrying me all day. I don't want people thinking I'm ungrateful, when they're just being kind."

The chance of getting into the cellar came early into the shift, when Julie was asked to collect some bottles of tonic water, Debs said she would keep an eye on the bar, sending her and Angela. She handed Julie the key. THE KEY!

"If you go together," Debs nodded. "It will be easier, and you can both carry more tonic and do it quicker than one."

Julie's heart leapt, she looked over at Angela.

"C'mon, love, we're on a mission…, for tonic water. Let's do this."

They couldn't get down the steps quickly enough. As they walked through the bar, Julie coughed slightly, looked over at Ned, and gave a tiny thumbs up, and pointed downwards. He gave a cursory look over and smiled.

"Everything going, ok?" He grinned. "Not working you too hard, are they? This book is getting really good. Think I might stay for another." Hardly smiling, he gave a wink, 'message received'.

"Right, I'll look for the door, and make a key mould," she said quickly to Angela, and you look for the tonic water as well as anything that resembles an opening. Julie took the key and pressed it firmly into the ball of plasticine that Ned had given to her. She felt elated, first task achieved. And perhaps the most important one.

Debs called down to the cellar, "I forgot to mention, the tonic water is at the far left in the corner."

"Thanks," they replied together. "Sorry Debs, couldn't see it for looking." Angela said jokily.

"Don't worry," answered Debs, "I had the same problem on my first day here."

For such a small room, there was a lot of stock and so many barrels and bottles of drinks that they'd never even heard of.

"Why don't you go to the right to look for a door, while I get the tonic water," whispered Angela. "I can take that up and you can follow, might keep Debs happy for a few minutes."

Making her way around the cellar looking for anything that would or could be any sort of opening, Julie felt so close to finding her sister but knew they were still so far away.

Angela called her to help, "Hey Ems, any chance of that tonic water? Or are you going to stay down there all night?"

"Hold your horses, I'm on my way." Julie knew exactly what Angela was doing. They mustn't cause any suspicion.

Raising her eyebrows questioningly as Julie came up from the cellar, Angela immediately realised that she hadn't found anything.

"These are heavy!" Julie explained, as she struggled to put the tonic water onto the bar.

She looked at Angela, momentarily showing her the impression of the key, and quickly putting it back in her pocket. She grinned, but only slightly. She'd got what they came for.

The shift went quickly. The best part for Julie and Angela was when the door opened, and a group of bikers walked in. They knew immediately this was Bill and the boys. Deb's face was a picture, horror mixed with an uncertain confusion. Angela dived straight in.

"Afternoon, Gents, welcome to The Gateway," smiling widely. "What can I get you?"

Despite the way Bill looked, it was clear there was no malice in him, nothing that you'd normally expect from a biker gang walking through the front door.

"Good evening, we just thought we'd pop in for a pint."

Even Angela seemed a little taken aback. Bill's voice was low, and his eyes were kind. She liked him immediately. And the small wink he gave her reassured her totally.

"Well, I can certainly help you with that," she laughed, "what would you like to drink guys?" she said easily. She glanced over at Debs and winked. 'Got this', she mouthed, and grinned. Debs smiled back, the relief was obvious.

"They're here," she whispered to Julie when she had a chance.

"Is it ok if we sit outside with those?" Bill asked politely. Every word that came out of his mouth surprised Angela. Looking at him with his rough and ready looks you'd expect a 'darlin' or 'treacle'. But he spoke like he had been well educated.

With the bikers milling around, Angela and Julie felt safe walking back to the campervan. Bill and the lads were clearly getting on well with the other campers.

"All alright?" Asked Ned, who had walked back with them.

"I like Bill," said Angela, simply, "he makes me feel safe."

"Yes," Julie replied. "And, I have the impression of the key." As she handed it to him.

"Perfect," he smiled. "Great job, Jules. I'll get a copy cut in the morning. Any luck in finding a door in the cellar?"

Julie and Angela both shook their heads.

"Nothing," Julie replied dismally. "And we must have been down there a good fifteen minutes looking for the tonic water."

"We really need to find that door," he said, clicking his tongue impatiently. His frustration was obvious.

"Is it possible that the door might not be there anymore?" Julie asked. "What if the passages are now closed off or caved in? What if Mandy is being held at Paul's Aunt's in one of the rooms above the Post office? Or Duro Rock or even at Ma's?"

"Yeah, I hear you, Jules," he replied, gently. "But remember your sister was staying at The Gateway after she had visited all those places, she may well have been drugged too. They would have needed to take her somewhere and you noticed a thread of her coat on the other side of the bar near the door hatch leading to the cellar. There must be a door there. I'll ask the boys to check out the map and see if they can give us some ideas."

"Where are you going?" Julie asked, shocked. Ned ignored her, tucking one of the maps into his pocket.

"Back shortly."

They both watched aghast as Ned went to the field with the map, asking 'the boys', what they thought of Duro. Standing in front of Bill's tent, he nonchalantly threw the copy in front of him. The movement was almost invisible.

"Well, it's a place to kick back. Only just got here, but I think the lads like it, right boys?"

He asked if they had any spare batteries, an innocuous question, just in case The Watchers or The Listeners were about.

"Yes, somewhere." Was Bill's amiable response, that's one thing we can rely on Skinny for." Lifting his head, he called over his shoulder, "hey Skinny, you got any spare batteries back there?"

A small voice came from somewhere back in the camp. "Plenty, just let me finish setting up."

"Where are you staying? We can bring some over to you when we find them."

"Brilliant, mate, I really appreciate it. Owe you a pint for that."

"In the scheme of things, it's nothing. You have a good night, and we'll try to keep the noise down." He grinned mischievously.

Ned returned hoping again it would cause no suspicion. The car park was empty, but who knew what might be watching from the shadows.

"Good news," he said, as he climbed back into the Rascal, "those guys have some batteries and are going to sort us out, when they finish setting up. Seems like a pretty decent bunch, actually." Immediately the doors were closed, his voice dropped. **"**We just have to wait now."

Angela made a pot of tea, as they sat and waited, still looking at the map to see if anything stood out or if there was anything they may have missed.

They didn't have to wait long as there was a tap at the window. Ned threw the door open.

There was Bill. A six-foot-plus man, with a greying bushy beard, shoulder length hair to match. Julie and Angela were both taken aback.

"Hello, mate, got those batteries for you. What sort did you need?"

"Come in," welcomed Ned. "Would you like to join us for a cup of tea?" He purposely left the back doors of the van open, so anyone watching would be able to see inside.

"Wouldn't say no." he replied easily, "love a pint, but you can't beat a good cuppa." He grinned as he sat on one of the trio of benches in the Rascal home.

"This is cosy." Then, rubbing his hands, he passed the map back to Ned as Angela poured.

He introduced himself as Bill, and he and Ned had been mates for years.

Julie laughed, "yes, we kinda guessed you were Bill." He smiled back, then ignored her.

"Well," he said, taking a deep breath. "The lads have taken a good look at the map after they read the book, all about Duro. We don't think there can be a door. There can't be, the river waters from The Duro run far too high to dig out a tunnel from The Gateway basement."

Looking at the disappointed faces he carried on, "If you look closely though to where the tunnel comes out at The

Pastures it seems to come up into a room. Maybe years gone by this room could have been an old pantry."

"And?" asked Ned, urgently.

Ned and Bill hunched over the map as Bill carried on talking. "You aren't looking for a door leading to a tunnel as such. It looks like you are searching for an old indoor well, which veers away from The River. So, you are looking for some sort of entry on the floor in the pub's cellar."

Julie butted in. "Mandy said that when she was shown a room over at Ma's that she had spotted an opening in the floor and had been told it was an old dried-up indoor well."

"Nice work, mate," smiled Ned, "really appreciate your help with this."

"By the way," Bill said, as he got up to leave. "We also noticed at the bar this evening that there are no security cameras in or around the pub; strange don't you think? Anyway, I'm off to get my beauty sleep. Thanks for the brew, Anna." And he disappeared into the night.

This was exciting news to sleep on. As always, Ned was up bright and early and had decided they would head out of Duro to get keys cut and splash out on a full continental breakfast.

After an enjoyable feed from a variety of sugared pastries, croissants with honey, fresh orange juice and a cafeteria of full roast coffee, they set about planning the next step of rescuing Mandy.

"Right, you two finish up, I'll be back in ten minutes." He walked away without another word. Ned soon returned looking extremely happy with himself carrying a bag of duplicate cellar keys.

"One for each of us," he said, giving them each a copy of the cellar key, one for Clive if and when needed, and one key for Bill."

Ned placed Bill's key in a bag along with the replacement batteries. They headed back to The Gateway car park deciding to keep a low profile.

"We don't know who or what is watching us in Duro, but I think we all agree that something is."

For the rest of the day, the three of them played card games, rummy was a favourite, drinking pots of tea and eating chocolate biscuits, until it was time to get ready for their shift. Talking quietly to Ned; Angela and Julie decided when they were next sent down into the cellar, which was usually their first job, they would be moving as many bottles and barrels as possible to try to find the opening **of** the well.

But that evening, to their dismay, the bar had already been restocked and there was no reason for either of them to go to the cellar.

Debs approached to say it had been very quiet today and it was going to be quiet again tomorrow, and they probably wouldn't be needed again until Thursday when there would be a coach load of pensioners arriving.

She must have seen the disappointment on Julie's face.

"Look," said Debs**,** "If anything comes up, I'll let you know, OK?" Debs added, "are you sure you wouldn't like to stay? Just for tonight? **So,** I can get hold of you if any extra work comes up?"

Angela fired back. "No, that's alright. We can pop in for breakfast daily and perhaps you could let us know then?"

Debs smiled politely, and replied that it was fine. Both Julie and Angela knew that wasn't what Debs had wanted to hear, just from the look on Deb's face that was obvious.
"Well, it was just a thought. See you tomorrow."
Returning to the Rascal, Julie was almost inconsolable, crying tears of frustration. Angela put her arm around her shoulder.   "C'mon game face on 'til we get back to the van."

"My poor sister," Julie sobbed, as she dropped onto the orange seating. "We have come all this way. We have people here to support us and help with the rescue. Somewhere Mandy is underneath the cellar, and the saddest thing is she has no idea. We are so close but still so far away."

Ned and Angela tried to console her, but it didn't work. They both knew anything they said would be lost and trite.

Bill popped over for the key and replacement batteries. He picked up the mood immediately.

"What's up?" he asked, peering over at Julie. Ned quietly updated him.

"Don't you worry, my darling. Something will turn up," he smiled, it was a comforting smile. "It will all come good in the end, and that's exactly what we're here for. We'll make sure you're ok."

Julie wasn't so sure, at this rate they would all get stuck here in this eerie place with no proof of anything and with no contact with the outside world anything could happen. She shivered at the thought.

But as luck would have it, something came up out of nowhere.

Ned suggested ordering breakfast at The Gateway that morning, Julie thought it was to make a point more than anything. There weren't many cars in the car park and the boats along the river were still in their moorings.

A few other people were at The Gateway eating breakfast, it was obvious that they were organising a trip over to The Rock.

"Morning all," Ned said, giving that easy smile. Most of them gave him the same warm welcome, and those who weren't used to this kind of genuine friendliness just looked and carried on eating, seemingly embarrassed that a stranger would address them directly. "If you're off to The Rock, you're in for a treat, it's beautiful."

Then, there was Debs.

"Morning, Debs, we're feeling extravagant, plus I can't be bothered to cook this morning. Can we order three of your fullest Englishes, please?"

Debs' smile faltered then came back, "Morning Ned, Emma, Anna, of course coming right up. Coffee or tea?"

"Always gonna be tea for me." Julie and Angela agreed.

135

They were just about to tuck into breakfast and a pot of tea, when Debs rushed up.

"I'm so glad you're here," she said, rushing her words out. "I'm sorry to interrupt your breakfast but is there any chance you two could help me out this morning, please? I wouldn't ask, but today everything seems to be going wrong?"

"Yes, of course," Julie answered, immediately. "What's up, Debs?"

"I've just found out we're having two coach loads arriving tomorrow and now a group of twitchers have turned up, and, to top it all, the cleaner has called in sick." She looked at them, almost begging, her ponytail moving nineteen to the dozen.

"Would you please come back here at 9:30 after breakfast and clean? Would you mind?" She looked defeated, having to ask someone for help.

"Yes, of course, we will, won't we Anna?"

"Anything to help," Angela nodded.

Ned got up to leave, he looked over at Debs. "Hash Browns are the best I've ever had."

Debs blushed. "The chef is in the back, in the kitchen." Debs carried on, as they got up to leave. "I'll have to leave you two on your own, though, as I've got to do the cash 'n' carry run which is a good twenty miles away."

"Can I help in any way?" asked Ned, immediately sensing an opportunity, "I can come with you and help with the cash and carry. Or stay here and clean the decking and the tables, I've finished my book, and as you've stolen my two partners in crime, I'm at a bit of a loose end, to be honest." He grinned.

"Would you?" Debs smiled. "It would be wonderful if you could help clean here."

"Happy to help," replied Ned. This was a bit of luck and now the opportunity had fallen into their hands and hopefully they would find Mandy.

"Thank you all, I really appreciate this." said Debs, a wave of relief flooding over her. "Ned, I'll make sure you get paid for your time."

"No need, Debs, but another plate of those hash browns would be very welcome." He winked mischievously.

Things had started to fall into place at last for them. Thought Julie.

They hurried to finish their breakfast, leaving Debs in a much brighter mood.

Arriving back at The Bedford their mood had lightened significantly, perhaps all feeling that chances were starting to open up, each one leading them closer towards their goal.

"This **is** perfect," said Ned quietly. "Finally, luck seems to be on our side."

"I'm so nervous," Julie said quietly, uneasy about the whole situation. "This suddenly seems too easy," she said. "I'm sure they must have suspected something. Or maybe we're just part of a plan to make us disappear." She turned to Ned, and he could see she was genuinely frightened, but said nothing.

"Jules, you're overthinking," replied Angela, quietly. "We have so much back up and now is the ideal opportunity to see if we can find Mandy. Today's the day!" She smiled what she hoped was a reassuring smile. She tried not to show how terrified she was herself.

With the duplicate key in their pockets and Clive's phone number, just in case they found a phone line that worked, and they needed help. If only they had definite proof of Mandy's whereabouts. That's all that Clive would care about, and the only thing that would get him back down here.

Debs showed Julie and Angela where all the cleaning products were kept and had run through with Ned the jobs needing to be done while she was out.

"All will be well." He smiled, grinning broadly.

"It should only be a couple of hours until I'm back. I don't like this part of the job." She said, "I'm so grateful, seriously, to all of you." It felt like the only real, genuine smile that they'd ever seen from Debs.

So are we, thought Julie, thinking it would be great if the opening to the old well would be where her sister was. They could get her out and be gone from this place before Debs returned. She hoped.

Bill and the 'boys' had been observing the pub and outside area as they had a few beers. They were polite and friendly. Not what you'd expect from a group of denim and leather clad bikers, at least not in this quiet backwater.

Ned was relieved there were no cameras or security as it made the plan easier.

"Morning," said Bill, lifting his beer in salutation, as they walked across the carpark.

"Hello, my friend," Ned hailed him back, "enjoying your stay? Get across to The Rock, if you get a chance. You won't regret it."

They waited for Debs to drive off. The three of them made sure the coast was clear before opening the cellar door. Ned stood guard, preparing his mop and bucket as they made their way downstairs to try and find the door they were looking for.

After a good twenty minutes of finding nothing, Julie sat on one of the barrels.

"This is not what we had planned at all, Debs will be heading back soon, and we haven't started any jobs yet. Let's just put this one down to experience, maybe we'll have better luck next time." She tried to smile but couldn't.

Angela and Ned reluctantly agreed.

"But" Ned said hesitantly, "there may not be a next time. How about if you stay down here, making room for the beer delivery or something. No-one's going to argue with that. Me and Angela can get on with the cleaning."

Julie had to admit that sounded like a good idea, and completely plausible, if anyone turned up unannounced.

As Angela took the steps returning to the pub, she stopped abruptly. She noticed behind the open stairs that in the floorboards there was a cut slightly out of line with the rest.

Without breath, Angela gasped.

"Come here, Jules, right now!" She pointed excitedly. "The entrance is there on the floor behind these steps. We found it! We finally found the entrance!"

Julie's mouth went dry, and her palms began to sweat. This is what they had come here for, but now it was actually happening she didn't know if she could do it. Her fear of the unknown froze her to the spot. Would she be able to deal with what she might find?

"Just think and keep your wits about you." Said Angela coming back down the steps towards Julie and the ominous lid to the passageway, and the secrets it might conceal. "You don't have to do anything when you're down there, ok? Just take some photos of evidence, that's if you can find anything. You may even find Mandy but may not be able to rescue her. If anything happens and you aren't back by the end of the day. We will get help."

"Not until the end of the day?" Julie asked, incredulously, "I'm not planning on being down there that long. I'm still not sure about this, Angela." If she was expecting some calming platitude from Angela, she certainly didn't get one.

"Look," said Angela snappily. "There's no one about at the moment you will be fine, now go while you can, this might be the only chance we get. I'll wait here and pretend to be doing stuff, I'll check the passageway every half an hour, and I'll keep Ned informed. He's keeping an eye out upstairs. You will be safe, I promise."
With those words they lifted the latch opening, there was a short flight of stairs, lit up and spacious.

"Go! Go now!" encouraged Angela. "It'll all be ok."

THIRTEEN

Julie hesitantly started to descend the stairs. Her heart in her mouth was pounding so loudly.

"Can you hear that, Angela?" Julie asked looking upwards. She could still see Angela's face, she tried to smile, but it didn't quite happen.

Julie tried to occupy her mind with the reality of the situation, and questions that she might be able to answer, rather than this continual 'what if, what if.' She nearly got to the bottom of the stairs and stopped. She was breathing heavily, not through exertion, it was straightforward naked fear.

What if she was caught and couldn't be found? What if she met someone in this tunnel, what would she say? More to the point, what if Mandy simply wasn't here?

Julie took one last look up, to see Angela smiling at the top, her thumbs up, she seemed to be so distant, and a lifetime away. Eventually, reaching the last step and finding herself at the start of what looked like an endless tunnel. In the corner was some sort of operating table with restraints.

Julie took a deep breath and thought she could hear voices which seemed to be close by.

What was she thinking, putting herself in this situation? She was weak and terrified. She had a choice. She really needed to think, either carry on with what they came here to do or go running back to Angela and Ned with her tail between her legs.

Feeling more vulnerable and alone than she'd ever felt, Julie took a step forward.

Julie stood for what felt a lifetime, staring at a dimly lit brick tunnel. It was damp and covered with mould. Moss covered the floor making it quite slippery in places. And constant unexpected drips from the ceiling were icy cold.

To the left there was a long line of black shapeless robes hung on hangers. With a feeling of dread, Julie inspected closer and suddenly realised what she was looking at. These robes belonged to The Watchers! So, there were people wearing these things roaming around. But for what? Trying to scare people away? She couldn't make sense of it. At least now she knew The Watchers weren't some sort of supernatural manifestation. Not that that really helped. Costumes trying to scare folks away. Why?

She couldn't wait to get back with the news.

To the right hanging up were the blue and white uniforms that she had spotted people wearing through the viewfinder when she had visited Duro Rock.

Julie took one of the uniforms off its hanger, it smelt clean. There was a sort of chemical smell that she knew but couldn't quite place, but at least if she wore one of these uniforms she would be in disguise and would hopefully blend in perfectly well with the rest of the workers.

From the little she'd seen so far, all she wanted to do was to get out of this place, she didn't feel safe. And, she hoped if something happened to her down here then someone would come and find her. She didn't want to be left down here, with no-one knowing what had happened. She just hoped she would be able to leave this place and would be rescued if not.

The operating table with restraints made her shudder. She couldn't imagine what went on here. She tried to push the thoughts away, she remembered what Angela had said, this could be their only chance. She had to continue the search and push these thoughts away. She so wanted Angela by her side. She could have put a Worker suit on too and no-one would be any the wiser. But Angela wasn't here. She thought back to what Ned had said to her about growing a pair. It made her smile, despite where she was. It would be ok, Angela and Ned knew where she was and would be here if she became imprisoned in any way.

From what she'd seen so far, she was pretty certain that everything was leading her towards Mandy.

Julie hurriedly put the long white dress on with the blue apron pulling the ties tightly around her waist. It was slightly on the larger side allowing her to keep her leggings and t-shirt on underneath. Attaching the bonnet and lower face covering she was now in total disguise.

Julie started her next part of her journey. Her footsteps followed her, the brick tunnel sending constant, disconcerting echoes as she quickly made her way.

Julie realised with unease that she must now be walking under The River Duro, it was a strange, stifling feeling, all that water just above her head.

The shadows stayed, always there. Although she knew they belonged to her, it wasn't comforting in any way. She was still nervous and on edge, and the constant dampness chilled her. Her mind kept telling her to turn back, as it had done so many times on this journey. Julie was still feeling apprehensive at what she might find when she eventually arrived at the end of this seemingly endless tunnel. Mandy had said the workers didn't talk, they just nodded, which she was thankful for. She didn't have their flat, toneless way of talking, with almost no emotion. Just the facts. Always saying as little as possible. She was glad Mandy had mentioned all of this to her.

Coming to the end of the passage, Julie arrived at a metal rung ladder. Checking she was still alone down here. She breathed another sigh of relief. So far so good. Looking up she saw a hint of light shining through what appeared to be an ill-fitting wooden lid.

Climbing up the rung, she'd never felt wearier. The steel was icy cold, although her palms were sweaty, as she neared the top the circular wall inside the well was very narrow and with her usual claustrophobic tendencies, she was sure, absolutely convinced, that everything was closing in on her. She lowered her head and took a deep breath. She was so close now she had to face her fear. Julie realised she had just had to lift the lid, and she would be at Ma's house. From what Mandy had told her, she knew she had just climbed up inside the dried-up indoor well and very soon she'd be entering the freezer room.

She was right. The room was cold and smelled sterile as Julie emerged from the tunnel. It wasn't a pleasant smell, it seemed to be masking something. Luckily, the room was empty, and the red quarry floor tiles helped to keep the room cool. Julie noticed many different types of freezers that filled the large storage space, mostly upright, and further to the back were chest freezers. Julie was scared. What *had* she walked into? Instinct told her that whatever it was, it wasn't good, and it certainly wasn't normal.

Julie had to open one, Mandy had said, although she hadn't got to see inside any of them, Ma had told her they were used for herb germination and pharmaceutical properties. Julie had to make sure. Mandy, had sounded more guarded than usual when she had mentioned this room to her almost like people were listening in to what she was saying.

As Julie slowly, nervously opened the nearest freezer, she felt bile rise from the pit of her stomach into her mouth. All she could see were many rows of frozen blood vials with numbers boldly written in marker pen.

What was going on here? Her mind couldn't begin to imagine what she was seeing.

"There you are," came a steely voice, making her jump. Julie slowly turned around and came face to face with two workers, dressed in the same blue and white uniform. "Ma has been looking for you."

"You are slightly late," said the other worker. "Ma doesn't appreciate tardiness." Julie didn't answer. She didn't know if they or Ma even knew who she was.

"Debs said you are a great cleaner and dedicated worker, she had sent a message to let Ma know you were happy with the job you had been offered with us Listeners. Kate, isn't it? Come."

They must think I'm Kate. Julie thought with relief, but with added concern of dread.

So, Julie thought these people in the long blue costumes were Ma's workers *and* 'The Listeners'.

Following the two Listeners, she hoped she wasn't being led into a trap. Neither of them said a word. The anxiety and uncertainty. The feeling of nausea was constant. As they walked Julie thought, she had to try to remember the route back, take photographs, and hopefully find Mandy.

Every fibre of her told Julie that her sister was here.

There were more corridors leading off into rooms, which Julie was frightened to look into, afraid of what she might see. Visions that might later come back to haunt her. Strange aromas and noxious odours were coming from everywhere. All angles. Workers passed carrying baskets of colourful flower heads. All in total silence, just a nodding gesture to show fellowship, that everyone knew what was really going on, and that they were all in this together.

Julie had lost all sense of where she was, or likely to be. She was desperately trying to envision the map in her head. She couldn't with so much fear and adrenaline, her mind was simply…, empty. Julie just hoped Mandy was here with Ma. Helping Ma and she could join them both.

FOURTEEN

The Listeners went through yet another door, leading to a small, cobbled courtyard. A beautiful lilac wisteria, its blooms hung like grapes clinging to the walls. The building looked like the farmhouse Jack had pointed out to her when she took the ferry from The Gateway to Duro Rock during her first visit, pointing out the building and saying the old farmhouse belonged to Ma.

The climber's fragrance was heavily scented replacing the underlying putrid smell that had been lingering in the corridor. Julie breathed in the sweetest perfume and as they walked towards the rambling old farmhouse's front door, she realised suddenly that for the first time she would be coming face to face with her grandmother, Ma.

Perhaps Mandy was trapped here against her will and had been talked into being a Listener. Or maybe she was happy here, just here helping Ma, because she wanted to.

The anticipation started to build inside her chest. Fight or flight uppermost in her tiny, frightened mind. She felt like a small mouse. And utterly defenceless. Whatever happened, this was Ma, her grandmother. Finally, what did she expect? She didn't know.

"You must be Katie?" a voice asked, as an elderly lady emerged into the hall. Julie nodded trying to focus and push the panic away. The decor around was of an ageing yellowed magnolia, cobwebs decorated the dark ceiling corners and paintings of corn stooks adorned the walls.

"You're late. We run a strict timetable here, I can't bear tardiness." She spoke in an accent that Julie couldn't place. It was accusatory, but not overtly unkind. Perhaps just slightly menacing.

"Don't talk, just follow. I don't like to talk, unless I have to."

Saying nothing, Julie followed her into a small room. A huge fireplace took up most of one wall.

"I hate to be cold, even on summer days I still feel the chill. I've always felt a chill, in my heart, and in my bones. I don't know why, exactly," she looked outside, distractedly, then turned her face suddenly towards Julie.

"Now, sit!" she commanded as she lifted her skirts and perched on the edge of the chair.

Julie sat. The matching sofa had certainly seen better days, it was a faded pink, moth-eaten and worn. Perfectly at home were a couple of purring black cats, Julie squeezed in as not to disturb them.

Julie took a sharp intake of breath, Ma looked so much like Mandy, her eyes blue and soulful. But her eyes never seemed to stay the same colour, constantly changing, almost like her moods. One minute friendly, the next harsh and almost attacking. Julie wasn't sure how to deal with these sudden mood swings. Mandy was so much like her, it was uncanny.

Julie wanted to run to Ma, hug her and let her know she was her granddaughter. But she couldn't, how could she? She had no real idea of the situation she was in, or even if Mandy was here. Was Ma her friend or foe? Julie wasn't certain.

"Debs has told me you would like to join our team and become a Listener?" said Ma, staring at Julie in a strange way, only Julie's eyes were visible from above the face mask she was wearing, and she was thankful for that.

"The Listeners keep a tight rein. They know that's what I expect. Debs said you love to clean, and you do a grand job over at the tavern. I don't need you to work on the farm, but twice a week to keep the lab house sterile, and three times a week I'd like you to mingle, doing your cleaning duties as normal, keeping your ears and eyes open and report to me on anything or anyone that stays there. Do you have any thoughts?" It was an innocuous question, almost asked as if she really cared, or was interested in the answer.

"You will have a bed here and food when you are on this side of Duro. The Watchers will keep an eye on the village in the evening." Julie nodded taking in all this information. What was the 'lab room'? she thought, but knowing she would soon be shown.

"You will be looked after well, there will always be a place for you here, at The Pastures."

A Listener joined them carrying a beautifully decorated silver tray transporting two beautiful silver goblets, and a large clear glass teapot filled with what looked like a large daffodil bulb, when boiling water was added. Julie watched with fascination as the bulb transformed in the teapot into a beautiful flower looking like a lily on a Lilypad and smelt of a profusion of jasmine, orchid and vanilla.

"We make this here," smiled Ma, "we sell it all around the world." She sounded proud of her achievements and poured them a goblet full each.

"You seem tense, this will take the tension from your body and relax your soul." Julie took a sip, and had to admit the taste was extremely soothing.

"Mmm, that's good," she smiled at Ma.

Ma almost smiled back. She wasn't good at smiles, not ones that you could believe, anyway. You smile with your eyes, but they never seemed to reach that far.

"I imagine you've never tasted anything like that before?" she grinned, showing beautifully white teeth and an almost wrinkle-free face.

Then, suddenly, out of nowhere, what Ma said next caught Julie completely off guard, and she almost choked on her tea.

Ma stood and walked to the window as she spoke.

"People say I'm a witch and use Wicca," she chuckled, but it was a sound that didn't quite work, "but I'm not and I don't. I have just been fortunate to have been raised here, with the monks and this beautiful land where I have studied animals, bees, butterflies and birds. Working alongside them I have built up an industry to help people with their ailments, and I've been able to do this all across the world. Hopefully, giving all a better life. More reason to live. And we all need a reason to live, don't we?"

She looked at Julie, it wasn't a question.

"Of course…, absolutely!" Julie answered enthusiastically.

Ma continued, "butterflies and moths are so underestimated. We need them more than people realise." Grinning emptily again, she said, "you could say we need them so much more than people. They are so important for flower pollination. I have grown an avenue of buddleia trees. The scent and sight of bees and butterflies when they come out in bloom brings happiness to my heart. And when I'm happy, it seems that so is everyone else. It's the balance we've reached here in Duro. And that's what I want to maintain."

Wow, Julie thought, the buddleia tree was Mandy's favourite plant too, she had planted one in remembrance of her sister's life, in her favourite place in the park.

Ma spoke again, taking her away from that particular thought. It was almost as if she knew when Julie was thinking outside Duro.

"Using petals from marigolds, carnations, lily roses, and from bamboo, and chrysanthemums. The perfume from orchid, jasmine, hibiscus and the list goes on." She sighed deeply, as if each word was a chore. "I infuse them and dry them into tea blossoms, to help people's minds and souls, similar to the one we have just shared.

At present, I am working on a project that I have been thinking about for many years. I stumbled on the idea by pure accident." She giggled like a little girl.

"And now, I might be closer than ever before. I'd try to explain it to you, but I don't think you'd fully understand my vision…, not at the moment, anyway. But you will." Again, her smile wasn't kind. It was just necessary to calm the lamb.

Again, Julie just nodded, mutely. All she wanted to ask was if she could stay here forever, tell Ma she wasn't Katie, tell her she was Julie, and be welcomed into the family. She wanted to learn more; she wanted to know everything Ma knew. She wanted a life here.

She was beginning to feel guilty and stupid, too. What had she been thinking, dragging Angela, Ned and his biker friends into this? It was a place that was beginning to feel safe to her.

The more Julie thought about it, she must have imagined it was her sister at the end of the phone, begging for help.
If anything, Julie could see how Mandy would be loving the life here. She'd always been such a free spirit, something that Julie envied.
Julie liked to believe Mandy was here, happily working the pastures amongst nature with Ma. There was a slight pang of empty jealousy, but something inside her, that churning of uneasiness stopped Julie from asking if Ma had seen Mandy and she was her sister. And had she heard anything about her disappearance.

Apart from everything that she'd been through over the last few hours, and the things she had learned, she still couldn't bring herself to ask the question. She had to admit to herself…, Ma scared her. Although she still wanted to be here.

There was a polite knock, and a man entered and butted into the conversation. Julie was taken aback to see a figure dressed in a long white coat, white wellingtons, gloves and a face mask.

"Sorry to interrupt, it's time Ma." She nodded and rose from her chair.

"Thank you," Ma smiled, looking down at her large wristwatch.

Julie wondered what 'it's time' meant, but she was soon shown.

"Follow me!" ordered Ma. "If your cleaning is as thorough as Debs tells me then I'll be teaching you how important it is that the room we are heading to is kept absolutely sterile," she looked hard at Julie, "this is possibly the most important room in The Pastures. Come, follow."

Swallowing hard, not sure what to expect, Julie did as she was told.

She was ordered to put on shoe protectors. The room they entered made her take a step back in horror, her breath caught in her throat. The white tiled floor was so clean she was sure you could have eaten food off it.

In the middle was a hospital bed, where an elderly man lay. His skin was so pale and transparent, Julie immediately thought she was looking at a living corpse. He had needles and tubes coming from his veins which were attached to monitors and machines showing various readings that she didn't understand.

Ma smiled a warm loving smile. It was the first real smile that she'd ever seen from Ma.

"And how is my darling man today?" She leant over to the frail man and kissed his forehead. "Are you ready?"

He didn't acknowledge her, but nodded, as she took his arm.

The worker followed them into the room holding a vial of blood with the number 427 written on the container. Ma linked the blood to a different machine and the blood slowly began to drip into his veins.

"Thank you," he said gratefully. He was obviously trying to smile, but it looked more like someone going through a paroxysm of absolute agony.

"Thank you, m'lovely." He smiled, then seemed to fall asleep. Again, Ma kissed him on his forehead. Seeing her show any kind of real emotion was unsettling. Julie turned away.

"I don't think there's much left in him, but we try and keep him as comfortable as possible," Ma suddenly broke in, "I just can't stand the thought of losing him," her voice hardened, something Julie was getting used to, "I will do anything and everything I can to make sure he can stay with me longer. You see, when he goes, I want to go too. I don't want to be here without him. Now do you begin to understand the importance of what I'm trying to do here?"

Julie looked at the body in the bed. She couldn't believe this was her grandad, Pa, who everyone thought had died years ago. She just stared, she couldn't juggle her emotions at that moment, so she just stayed silent.

"Like I said," said Ma, turning directly to Julie, "I am searching for eternal youth. This is my husband, the love of my life and unfortunately, he was born with the golden blood, the blood of the gods. You will not say a word about anything you see here. Is that clearly understood?" Her stare chilled Julie to the bone. She nodded. Ma continued to stare at her for a moment. "These rooms are your responsibility."

"Just this room?" Julie's voice was meek.

"Oh no! Follow. There is the freezer room, where the blood is kept. That can wait, really. It's just blood, and all blood is red. This is just to make sure we know who it belongs to. We need to make sure it goes to the right guest. Then, there's the next room." She grinned but said nothing. She didn't even look at Julie. "This literally, is the life blood."

Julie's head was spinning, her heart was pumping, she didn't want to see another room. She just wanted to get back to Angela and Ned, Bill and his mates. Again, she just nodded at Ma, and as always, followed.

Ma stopped so suddenly that Julie almost bumped into her. For some strange reason, she didn't want to touch Ma. An hour ago, all she'd wanted was to throw herself into her arms and tell her who she was. Ma turned and grabbed her arm; she was surprisingly strong for an elderly lady.

"I don't go into the next building. Despite its importance to the whole venture, there's something that I find distasteful about it. I simply think of it as the guest wing. The white coat man will show you what to do and what is required to keep this part of the building absolutely sterile at all times. I'll speak to you again when you have been shown your tasks." Without another word, she turned and walked away.

Following the white coat man, Julie noticed he had now put a white plastic apron over his overalls and passed one to her.

"You might need this." He spoke without a hint of emotion.

"What for?" Julie blurted out, startled.

"You'll see…, but hopefully you won't." The response didn't really answer her question. "It all depends on whether they've harvested yet today. *That* is definitely a shift you want to avoid."

Julie wanted to ask more, but thought that might cause suspicion, so she kept her thoughts and questions to herself.

The white coat man as Ma had called him, beckoned to Julie as he lifted a large flagstone tile in front of them and started to descend steps, which were extremely steep and dimly lit. They entered another tunnel. This one was a lot shorter than the previous one. As they walked further, Julie started to pick up the same sickly-sweet chemical smell as she had earlier. It seemed to grow stronger with every step. But smell wasn't the right word for it. Stench described it better. It was thick and cloying, and Julie thought she might vomit.

As they approached the end of the dark dank tunnel Julie looked up to steps leading into darkness. The white coat man never spoke or turned to make any gesture. Julie solemnly followed, looking about her, she noticed peeling paint and black mould spores.

The man knocked at a door hidden in the shadows, Julie's first thought was that she was to be thrown into a dungeon of sorts.

So, she gasped with shock when the door opened. An extremely bright light shone through.

They walked into a room looking like some sort of laboratory kitchen. There were smells, but nothing that was inviting. Whatever was being cooked here was medical, and not something that would be consumed for pleasure.

Julie looked up and saw windows at the top of the building, allowing natural light through. She noticed on one side growing tall and reaching the window was the sweet, scented dog rose and wild honeysuckle. The other three sides showed barbed wire.

She remembered Mandy mentioning this barn to her. Ma had shown Mandy the outside and mentioned it was a place she had never ventured inside. No wonder Mandy had said she hadn't noticed an entrance. There wasn't one. You could only enter this place by tunnel.

Here, every worker wore white coats and looked like laboratory technicians. They were cooking foods and broths, which had absolutely no aroma. This was food that was to be eaten by someone who didn't care what they had put in their mouths. They didn't ask for what they wanted; it was decided for them.

The plastic bowls and cups were all numbered, in bold black numbers. All labelled with numbers which matched the same ones Julie had spotted in the freezer room.

There were centrifuges, seemingly endless rows of chemicals, syringes, cotton wool, and kidney trays piled high. Amongst surgical instruments that she really didn't like the look of.

The white coat man turned to look at her.

"When we enter the next room, you don't stare at the projects." He ordered in the same tone as Ma's.

Bemused, Julie asked, "what projects?"

"You'll see soon enough. You just keep your eyes on the floor. Just look at the floor where we clean, and the bars, always make sure the bars are clean. You will soon get used to it, and it will make things easier for you. Believe me, it makes things easier for all of us. Finish your shift, go home and try to convince yourself this isn't happening. I think I've said enough."

He turned and wheeled in a large trolley of different cleaning chemicals, sponges and mops, with bin liners tied on the side.

Following him through into the main building of the barn, music was playing 'Theme from a Summer Place' which was being played on repeat, Julie found this annoying.

Although wearing a mask the smell wafted through the covering, and she stifled back a heave. Julie could not take in or believe it when she saw where she was. What was she looking at?

There were cages on each side with people in them, the numbers she had noticed earlier matched and were written above their cell doors.

Ma had told Mandy she didn't believe in animal research. She was researching on humans instead! Julie looked around as the white coat man began unloading the cleaning products and explaining what and where each product was to be used. She wasn't listening, almost crying out in horror when she saw Jack in one of the cages. A number was written above his cell along with his blood type, and his dietary requirements.

Then there was Paul, lying comatose in another cell. His eyes were open, but it was easy to see he wasn't there, well, not in any real sense of the word. He was smiling. And drooling, the spit was running down his chin. Having known

Paul, it was a disgusting thing to see. Above his cell was simply written RH Null.

A small bomb dropped in Julie's stomach. Paul was also carrying the golden blood, one of the chosen ones. Had he known? No wonder he had never returned any of her calls, he'd been here, rotting in a living coffin.

"They've all been milked." Said the white coat. "So, let's just do what we need to do and get out of here."

Julie knew this was bad, she knew this was terrible. People who had gone missing were here at Ma's for her to experiment on!

A thought crossed Julie's mind; she was wondering if Paul's aunt was also involved in this.

She looked across to the other side of the barn where more cages were slightly set back, there was a woman who caught Julie's eye, she looked like Susan, her blank-looking face matched the missing photo. The sign hanging on the cage was also RH Null.

Most of them were either sleeping, or just staring at nothing. All wearing white vests and matching shorts.

Julie looked around knowing that Mandy was here. She didn't know how, she just knew. She could almost sense her presence. And, suddenly, there she was in the end cell. Julie's sister Mandy, the number 427 the blood vial used for Pa earlier on matched her cell number. Mandy must have the golden blood too.

Julie wanted to catch her attention, and rush over and hug her and let her know she was there to rescue her, although she wasn't sure how. Such a massive rush of emotions. Her sister was alive! How? she didn't know or care. She was there, right in front of her eyes. It was Mandy, but it wasn't. She stared at Julie, but there was no recognition. Their eyes met, she smiled at Julie, but nothing was behind it.

Despite her excitement, she knew she had to remain calm and try to stay focussed.

"Try to work faster," said the white coat man as he interrupted her euphoria, making her jump. "And don't stare. Ma doesn't like it if we stare."

"Who are these people? Why are they here?" she asked, trying to sound naïve.

"Oh, they're just called guests. No-one knows, and we don't ask."

She easily disregarded his ominous words. Julie's heart was doing cartwheels. Her sister was alive! Julie averted her eyes so as not to stare and tried to up her speed.

FIFTEEN

How Julie wanted to catch Mandy's attention, and to let her dear sister know she was there to rescue her, although she wasn't sure how?

Nobody called out or tried to escape as they had their blood taken.

She couldn't help noticing the clipboards outside the cages. On each was written different diets and pills to be administered throughout the day. She looked, surreptitiously at them but nothing made any sense to her, it was like a foreign language.

Julie tried so hard to take photographs with her phone but there was no such luck. With cameras at every corner, she simply couldn't take the risk.

"We are finished here for now." Said the worker Julie followed him into the utility room next to the kitchen and all the cloths were put into a strong disinfectant. She was so relieved to remove the gloves and apron. After what she's just seen, and done, they made her feel unclean.

She was hoping to be released from this place of Ma's and desperately wanted to get back to Angela and Ned. She convinced herself she would never be coming back. After what she'd just witnessed, she knew this was definitely a job for Clive. Now, just the thought of getting out of here safely was her main priority. She couldn't focus on anything beyond that. There really was no plan, so she knew it could be a major problem. Her mind was racing, and her heart was struggling to keep up.

Ma came to meet Julie smiling.

"The white coat man has reported back to me, saying what a great asset you will make. I look forward to seeing you here, Kate, in two days as a Listener." She smiled her usual emotionless smile.

"Over the next two days in Duro I would like you to listen out and around in The Gateway, especially the conversations between the two new girls who arrived last week, Emma and Anna. My nephew who owns The Gateway, you may have been introduced to him as ol' man Salturns. Apparently, the girls have refused to stay there at the old tavern and have bought a campervan along with a guy called Ned. I want you to find out as much as possible about the three of them." She looked at Julie, her bright blue eyes looking straight into Julie's soul.

She stepped back and smiled. "If you do well, I'll promote you to helping me on the land, as I'm getting older, I'm looking for staff who are bright and take an interest here."

Julie smiled. "I would love to do that, to be your right-hand."

"I'll see you here in two days, hopefully with news. Go careful!"

A Listener came and collected Julie and walked back with her through the tunnel. Julie now felt a lot calmer, remembering to focus on what she was looking at, what she had seen, so she could tell Angela, Ned and Bill everything. She wanted everyone to leave Duro as soon as possible, after what she'd seen and been told today, she wanted everyone safely out of harm's way. This was something more than they were and it needed to be dealt with officially. Clearly, what Ma was doing was horrific and illegal. Surely. This was a job for Clive, and maybe this time if she had Angela and Ned backing up her story, he might actually listen.

"That's my shift over too," chuckled The Listener, taking off her overalls and hat and hanging them up.

"You can hang yours up next to mine if you like? They are all washed in the evening."

Julie looked at her, recognising her straight away from the Post Office the day she'd collapsed. She averted her eyes hoping she wouldn't have been recognised or even worse still The Listener knew Kate who cleaned at The Gateway pub.

"Ooh Kate," smiled Aunt's friend. "You look familiar, isn't it strange that us Listeners all look the same and work in silence and yet not wearing these costumes we become ourselves again."

"I don't think we have met," Julie answered.
The lady smiled, "perhaps we bumped into each other in the village shop?"

Julie ignored the comment and hoped the woman hadn't picked up her awkwardness of not answering. They walked in silence and took a different route taking them to a staircase which led to a back room of The Gateway.

Julie's body was full of adrenaline and her heart was racing.

She was so close to getting back to the Rascal, and blessed safety. Knowing her friends would be worrying about her by now. If anything happened to her *here*, she doubted she'd ever be found. That was a truly terrifying thought.

"This is the escape room," laughed The Worker. She laughed, when she saw the worried look on Julie's face. "We are now officially free from The Warren, which us Listeners and Watchers call the tunnels. "We can only exit this way." They walked out of the back entrance of The Gateway and into the car park.

Julie took a deep breath, she thought the air had never smelt so sweet.

"Now remember to listen into conversations and only report back to Ma." Smiling a friendly, but empty smile.

"Here in Duro, you'll find the best and safest place to be is in Ma's good books." She got into a car and headed off.

Julie felt like she had woken up from a dream, and a bad one at that. But, walking across the dusty car park, with the sun setting over Ma's land, The Pastures full of birds, bees and butterflies enjoying their busy lives, everything natural and thriving, enjoying their life in a proper balanced environment.

Dusk was falling, and she knew she had to get back to the Rascal before Ned decided to call for back-up. She needed to relay everything she'd witnessed. She hadn't been able to take any photographs, so she still had no actual evidence.

Over to the right of the car park, someone had emptied their ashtray full of cigarette butts, and crisp packets among a few plastic bottles and tin cans were littered about with no care or a thought. A decaying rabbit carcass was on the side of the hedgerow, a remnant of roadkill. A few dandelions and willowherb were trying to grow and establish roots, their leaves black, choked by car carbon fumes.

Julie tapped on the side of the Rascal.

"I'm back," she called, quietly.

The door flew open, Angela literally yanking her inside.

"Oh my god, you are back!" She kept repeating, hugging Julie hard.

Ned stuck the kettle on and grinned his pearly white smile.

"Glad you're back safe, kiddo, we were worried and about to drive off and report to Clive and get Bill and the boys ready for action."

Julie sat down and once the tea was brewed and Bill had joined them, she told them everything, as they all listened intently Julie couldn't let Clive or anyone else know what was really going on in The Pastures. After what she'd seen today, she felt almost as if she'd had an epiphany.

Although she knew the human experiments were way beyond wrong, she believed that Ma was giving the world new drugs and Mandy needed to be there to be kept alive.

Ma would give her the correct drugs and transfusions which she would need. Ma had obviously researched the golden blood, and its rarity, she obviously understood what was required for each 'guest'.

All the people who were caged all seemed to be in a good place. Whether it was right or wrong, if she stepped in to stop it, what would happen to Ma's land? Would it be bulldozed for houses or flats? The habitat of the insects that homed here and relied upon the flora would be no more and the fauna would die. It certainly wouldn't be kept as it was, no one had the experience that Ma had, she had been born and bred here, there was no one else to take it on apart from her, Julie, her granddaughter.

Julie began her story with all listening intently.

"It's an absolutely amazing place, and Ma, my grandma, is the most wonderful person ever."

Julie stopped to take a breather and sip her tea.

"Mandy wasn't there, Ma told me she believed she'd drowned. I'm so sorry to have dragged you all down here on a wild goose chase. But with all the pills and nightmares, I'm sure I just imagined Mandy calling and asking for help. Now I know for certain, and I have to deal with the reality that she's never coming home."

Angela smiled sympathetically, but looking relieved that Julie had eventually accepted that her sister was dead.

"Well, at least we tried, and I have to be honest, I don't like this place and I'll be happy to get home to some sort of reality…, and my bed."

Throughout the conversation, Ned had said nothing, sitting quietly, head down, looking at his hands.

Julie nodded with relief. They believed her.

"Right, we will be off then, Ned," said Bill standing up and slurping the last dregs of his tea. "Cheers guys, great to meet you all." Then looking at Julie, he said, "I'm glad you are ok, and finally managed to meet your grandma. Sorry about your sister, but at least now you can try and rebuild your life again, no matter how painful that's going to be. Stay well." He gave Julie a bear hug and said goodbye.

Bill left and Julie heard him call his mates, after half an hour their tents were gone, and with a roar of their motorcycles they drove out of the car park.

"Let's get out of here," said Ned. "I don't want to be here any longer than is absolutely necessary."

Julie smiled secretly to herself, things were working out better than she'd hoped. It was good to know that her friends wouldn't be dragged into whatever Ma was doing over in The Pastures.

"So, what was your grandma like? Did she show an interest in you?" Enquired Ned as he turned the Rascal round and headed out of The Gateway car park for the last time.

Angela felt a massive weight lift from her shoulders as they drove out of Duro.

Breathing a sigh of relief, she said, "this is one place I never want to visit again!" she giggled self-consciously.

"Yes, she was lovely," Julie said, finally answering Ned's question, "exactly what you'd expect from a grandma. It felt like I'd known her for years. She showed me around, it was just so impressive seeing what she's doing with nature all around here."

Saying nothing, Ned and Angela exchanged glances. Julie smiled to herself, as she began to drowse. She knew what she was doing was wrong but, after what she'd seen, she simply couldn't help herself.

SIXTEEN

It was good to be home.

Over the next two days, Julie told Angela she just needed some time and space to rethink things and decide what she was going to do next. Obviously, Angela respected her wishes. Ned came round to say goodbye.

"It's been an absolute pleasure meeting you, Jules, I'm sorry things didn't quite work out as we'd hoped. I'd like to say I enjoyed the few days down in Duro, but I think that would be a lie, wouldn't it?" He gave her his typical 'Ned' grin and hugged her, "you stay strong, and hopefully I'll see you again soon."

"What's next for you, Ned?" Julie asked and meant it. "What's your next adventure?"

"North, I think, quite fancy some mountains, not sure I ever want to see just rolling fields ever again."

"I'll miss you," she said, as he walked towards the door.

"Most girls do," he lifted a hand, and was gone.

Julie sat down on the sofa, feeling lost and empty. She looked around her. What next? She knew that Ma needed her help supporting her and taking over The Pastures one day. Surely, she'd be happy to meet another grandchild, someone who understood the great work she was doing.
Against her better judgement, she'd decided to go back to Duro, and go undercover as a Listener, until she felt she

could reveal who she really was. Hopefully Ma would understand and welcome her with open arms.

At last, Julie found herself in a good place mentally. She had a clear plan. She packed, ready to catch the earliest train which would take her back to Duro. She pushed a letter under Angela's door as she left. She hoped it would explain everything, and that Angela would understand.

She finally arrived at The Gateway.

Julie had to time it right and wait until Debs had gone to check on Kate who had come back to work after her bout of sickness. Kate was cleaning the rooms upstairs. Creeping into The Gateway, Julie made her way straight to and under the bar and with the key in her pocket opened the latch. She made her way down the steps into the cellar, closing the door quietly behind her. Lifting the lid, she descended hesitantly into The Warren.

The Listeners' uniforms were hung up, but this time there was only one uniform, which was lucky, otherwise she would have been stuck without a plan.

The operating table and tools were still in the corner which chilled her but, now Julie understood what was really happening here she brushed her fear aside, assuredly making her way through the tunnel, she knew she had made the right decision.

Julie soon found herself at the bottom of the old indoor well, as she confidently made her way up the steps into the freezer room she saw another Listener.

"Hi," she said. "Can you tell Ma, Kate is here please?"

The Listener nodded, wordlessly, and placed a tray of pollinators into a chest freezer, left to let Ma know of her return.

As Julie waited, she envisaged herself inheriting all of this. She smiled smugly to herself.

"Kate!" said Ma, suddenly appearing. "How wonderful to see you again, so prompt too." She smiled and nodded. "Come, follow."

Julie went without question.

She trailed Ma in silence through the hallway of pictured corn stooks, and into her room, the same cats were asleep on the sofa.

As Julie sunk down into the sofa, she heard cawing. Something she definitely didn't expect.

"Meet Crow, I just rescued him." A huge black crow demonic looking with his black piercing eyes and huge beak. He hopped onto Ma's shoulder. "Come here Crow," she said, stroking his head, and smiling as she looked at Julie with her smooth face and twinkly blue eyes.

"Do you have any news on the drifters in the Bedford?" Ma questioned. "The two women didn't appear on shift at The Gateway this evening. I just wondered if you knew of any reason why that might be?"

Julie looked at the crow on her shoulder and swallowed before answering, suddenly feeling extremely uncomfortable.

"I'm not sure." Julie replied, trying to hide the tremor in her voice. This conversation was definitely not going the way she'd expected. "I did notice their van isn't in the car park, though."

Ignoring her, Ma pointed towards the coffee-stained table where there was a clear glass teapot. A yellow tea blossom had already been poured into her cup.

"And... a surprise for you Kate, a new tea blossom for you to try." Ma reached forward and placed the bloom into the silver tea strainer and poured hot water onto the flower.

A dark indigo colour drained from the strainer and the flower looked like a purple lily.

Ma picked up the teapot as the brew flowed into a cup and she passed it over to her.

"Here, sip, I think you'll really like this one." Despite feeling nervous, Julie leaned over and took the cup from Ma.

The tea tasted of liquorice with highlights of blackberry. Although Julie wasn't a fan of liquorice, the taste was amazing.

"Nice?" Ma asked, looking intently at Julie. It was strange, she felt like Ma's eyes were trying to peer into her soul.

"Oh Ma, that's really good," she said enthusiastically.

Ma smiled enigmatically, "Good, I'm glad you like it. Now, drink up, there's plenty more if you want it."

Julie's head immediately began to feel slightly woozy, drunk almost.

"So, who are you today? Julie or Emma or Kate?" Asked Ma, with slight sarcasm. "You see I know you are not Kate as she visited me the day after I met you. She had been sick and so couldn't make that day when you turned up pretending you were her…but I knew that. I had The Watchers and The Listeners keep a very close eye on you and your friends. I know who you are, Julie and the damage you want to cause here."

"No, no," Julie heard herself say in a voice that wasn't hers. It was distant and echoed in her head. "No, you've got this all wrong," she gasped, a vague panic setting in, she slowly realised what Ma had just said to her. Whatever was in the tea had made her feel very strange. Totally disconnected.

"You, young lady." said Ma sternly, her voice totally changed, as she stood up, walking towards Julie, seeming to loom over her.

"I know you've been here before trying to find your sister. When you stayed at The Gateway, a blood sample was taken from your heel. Unfortunately, my dear, you don't have the Golden Blood."

"Firstly, you upset my very best friend, Aunty, even though she was trying to help you. But then to add insult to injury, you still kept poking your nose, and even worse… you brought outsiders into the village. Quite simply unacceptable, my dear." Even in her fuddled state, Julie sensed Ma growing angrier and angrier. The crow flapped his wings belligerently, and Ma's shadow became blacker, and seemed to grow.

"Paul's mother passed away when he was young. She had the golden blood. Aunty wasn't sure, but guessed that Paul would have it, too, so she sent him away, so I couldn't use him in my research experiments.

But when he returned and started meddling, Aunty had no choice but to hand him over to me. I always let Aunty deal with things, until they start to get out of hand. Then, I step in. I'd have found out, anyway. Luckily, I found out that Paul had the Null gene, and a very pure strain, stronger than I've ever seen, almost as pure as Pa's. I had to have that. Such a shame, a very handsome boy. Then, Paul decided to get poor innocent Jack involved. Snooping., but not for me."

"You must try to understand, Julie, although I know by now there can't be much of you left in there, which is what I hoped. Aunty and I had to put a stop to all this prying. Duro has always looked after itself, and I intend to keep it that way. Yes, you may look at me wide eyed, which you would do, if your eyes still worked properly. But they don't., do they?" A blurred, spiteful face came towards her.

"Aunty is my partner in this enterprise and between us we own the land and two thirds of the pharmaceutical company along with Duro Rock. It was great when Paul came up with your escape plan, you being Jack." Ma threw her head back laughing, sinister.

"Jack and Paul told everyone they were going to Wales and had no idea of their return, it was so easy for The Listeners to slip into local conversation that Paul and Jack had decided to live there. It was so easy for Aunty to drug them and cell type them. No one would wonder where they had disappeared to. Aunty and I try to only use people who are on their own, drifters or loners where they would never be missed. Obviously, villagers are different. They're terrified of The Watchers and The Listeners and have grown used to never talking to anyone about them, not even between themselves, and certainly not outsiders.

Jack, a normal blood type, but still of use. He helped willingly enough…, in the end.

Then when Paul returned telling Aunty that you had contacted that detective again, we knew we had to act."

Her voice dropped, and she suddenly sounded sad. From the harsh accusatory tones of the moment before, to someone simply reminiscing on times past.

"As you know, me and Pa married young. He was always a very sickly man. When we came to live here, there were still monks around. They tried various potions and tinctures to try and help him, but nothing seemed to work.

And then one of the monks concluded that it was his blood that was making him sick.

Of the four children we bore, two were special, the others just born with usual blood types. So, I had them adopted, not realising at the time how useful they could still be. I would need the golden blood for transfusions, although not exactly golden, there were still traces. So, when Susan and then your sister Mandy turned up looking for me, it turned my world around, and now I can help them and Pa. It opened a new door of opportunities for us, and the business. Over the years of trying to find a cure and help him, I have found other doors have opened for me to make more pharmaceutical products. So, I can use other people without the golden blood type to further my experiments.

I have Paul, and I'm not sure that Mandy realises how important she is."

"Thanks to you, you witch, Mandy doesn't know who she is, anymore!" Julie screamed. She knew she'd said it but wasn't sure whether the words had come out properly. They sounded jumbled.

"Oh, she knows who she is, but not exactly where she is. Last time you were here on your little 'rescue mission', you were fortunate enough for me to let you go. I have already discussed that little 'oversight' with Debs. But, not this time, my dear. You will still be helping me, but just not in the way you were expecting. You're young and healthy, so will be of use for what I am doing here.

Ma brought her face close to Julie's. Her breath was stale and old, like sand. All the colour drained from her eyes. All Julie could see were the pupils, an empty and depthless black. Ma brought a hood over her head.

Speaking in Gaelic, she stared straight at Julie. Her crow cawing, still on her shoulder flapping its black wings. It sounded like he was laughing. She felt a cold, bony hand on her forehead.

And, after everything, just those eyes. Julie thought…,

"BEANNACHT DE ORT-
(BAN-UKHT DAY ORT)
SLAN AGUS BEANNACHT
(SLAWN OG-US BAN-UKHT)
BEANNACHT DE LEAT
(BAN-UKHT DAY LAT)
BEANNACHT DE ORAIBH."
"GOD'S BLESSING ON YOU. GOOD-BYE AND BLESSINGS. GOD'S BLESSINGS WITH YOU."

Darkness.

EPILOGUE

Julie heard birds singing, and in the background the music was softly playing 'Theme from a Summer Place' on repeat.

She wondered if she was dreaming but opening her eyes, reality began to slowly sink in. Coming to, Julie really wished she wouldn't.

A sickly-sweet smell filled the air, looking down she saw she was wearing a white vest with matching shorts, looking up Julie saw the barbed wire looming up against the windows, creating shadows in the bright sunlight outside. The thought of the outside, so close, but a million miles away.

Looking across from her cell, the one she had cleaned two days prior, was Mandy, she'd been moved to the cage opposite, so they could see each other, although Mandy was too comatose to notice. Julie couldn't help wondering whether this was out of spite or meant to be a kind gesture. She guessed it was meant to be spiteful. She didn't think Ma had a kind bone in her body. At least if Mandy ever 'came back', she'd be there to see it, and her again.

Unfortunately, Julie knew there was no chance anyone was going to them. She'd drawn Angela, Ned and Bill into the search for her sister, then just walked away from them all.

And all because of her greed. What had possessed her? Why would she think that Ma wanted her as part of her family?
What have I done? Julie thought, knowing no-one would ever try and rescue them, why would they? The note she'd left for Angela made it clear what her plans were.

A white coat man came towards Julie with a kidney shaped tray, some empty vials, a needle and a tablet with a tea blossom.
Looking at her in the cage.

"Number 523," he smiled. "Just a little something to make your stay a little more comfortable."

AND FINALLY…

A big thank you to Mark, the editor of this book and author of poetry anthology *Cacophony*.

Elizabeth Moss is the pen name of Sarah E. Warne – author of "Lost Summers" and "Summer Rainbows" – both of which are sequels to "That Summer" – a fascinating memoir of wartime evacuation by Sarah's mother, Jussie E. Lilliot.

The aforementioned books are all available to order from www.vbay.com.

Printed in Great Britain
by Amazon